THE ISLAND OF THE SHEE

THE ISLAND OF THE SHEE

A.W. Strawsburg

ARPress
ILLUMINATING IDEAS.
EMPOWERING VOICES

ARPress
45 Dan Road Suite 36
Canton MA 02021
Hotline: 1(888) 821-0229
Fax: 1(508) 545-7580

Ordering Information:
Quantity Sales. Special discounts are available on quantity purchases by corporations, associations, and others. For details, contact the publisher at the address above.

Printed in the United States of America.

ISBN-13	Paperback	979-8-89330-318-6
	eBook	979-8-89330-319-3

Library of Congress Control Number: 2024900816

Acknowledgments

I would like to thank all of my family and many friends who have been so supportive of me and my writing endeavors. In particular, I would like to thank Jeri Hinkle for getting the book into a legible state. Thank you, Jeri, for all of your help.

I would also like to thank Michael Beenenga of Artistic Gold Creative Concepts, for the cover of the Island of the Shee. His creation is a brilliant portrayal of the characters in the book.

CHAPTER 1

Johnathan sauntered out of the plantation house. Riders with their horses pulled carts of sugar preparing their goods for market. This was the only life that he had ever known, inhaling the early scent of the flowers mixed with air was a common occurrence, but one that he never tired of. At seven years old, he could not imagine the world to be any different. At a small table in the shade, his father was talking to his uncle.

"Jamie, this is one of the best crops we have ever had. And now with your new ship, it's time to take the sugar to market. When are you going to be ready to sail?" His tone indicated his desire to rush to the market.

"John, the day after tomorrow, at high tide. I'm going to take a walk down to the dock this morning and check on the ship's progress."

"Why not take a horse, it would be faster," John said, betraying his desire for haste.

"Soon I will be at sea. I would like to enjoy the walk while I can."

"Jamie, I think I know someone who would like to walk with you."

"Johnathan?" Jamie asked.

With a smile, John replied, "He is going to miss you this trip. Maybe you could explain to him why you have to go."

"Johnathan is just about the most important person in the world to me. If I have a son someday, I hope that he is just like Johnathan. I would be happy to take him on my walk. Let's go get him." The two men started to walk back to the home. Johnathan saw them as he was always on the lookout for his uncle. He admired his uncle with a passion that exceeded love and was proud of the bond that had always existed between them.

"Uncle Jamie, I have been looking for you." Expecting a big hug, Johnathan ran for his uncle.

"Johnathan, how would you like to go down to the harbor town with me?"

"Father, can I go?" The boy searched his father's face for evidence that this excursion plan would be met with permission and love.

"First, ask your mother. We don't want to get Maria upset with us do you." Johnathan took off running, returning shortly with his mother.

"John, what is this I hear about Johnathan going down to the docks. Whose idea was that, as if I didn't know?"

Jamie, deflecting the question and taking most of the blame replied, "Now Maria, John, and I thought since I will be leaving soon that Johnathan would like to spend a little time with me."

Johnathan was surprised to learn of his uncle's plan to leave so soon.

Maria took Johnathan's arm. "Young man, I don't want you talking to the ladies by the docks, understand."

Johnathan nodded his agreement to the terms that his mother had sat down, while Maria glared at Jamie, "And don't scare him with those stories of yours."

Jamie waved, "We best be going." They walked to the end of the plantation. And started down to the town.

"Johnathan, I have a feeling that we are being watched." The hair on the back of his neck had risen to attention, but he was unaware that on the side of the jungle, lying close to the ground were eyes watching their every move.

"Uncle Jamie, tell me about the island that scares you."

"No, that I cannot do. Your mother would have a fit."

CHAPTER 2

As soon as Johnathan and his uncle were out of sight, the jungle became active with strangers struggling as quietly as possible. "Stay low until Captain James is out of sight. That will be one less we have to deal with," opined the scruffy man to his equally scruffy companions.

One of the pirates said to the other. "Tell, Captain LeDuval to bring more men. It is a very good day for a raid." Down the mountain, he went to a waiting ship in the cove, camouflaged and out of sight. He scaled down the mountain, taking time not to fall as he descended. Upon arrival at the pirate ship, the pirate captain demanded, "Well, man, is it worth our time?"

"Mr. Tom said to bring the men."

After a fair amount of time, the pirate ship emptied onto the shore. As usual, they were quick and quiet as-pirates know how to stay alive. It took the best part of the morning before they were ready.

They waited for the right time to strike. They hit the plantation house first. Hardly anyone was in it, just a few servants. When one pirate went upstairs, he surprised a woman making the beds. She screamed as loud as she could. Maria was outside talking to her husband. She turned toward to house.

"Pirates! We are under attack."

John grabbed his sword and pistol. "Maria, take the sword."

She caught it with one hand. She ripped her dress as she ran for the house. To the surprise of the first pirate coming out of the house, carrying some of her treasures, she moved the blade alongside his face. "The next cut I'm afraid I will remove your head. And as you probably know, heads are a lot harder to put back than they are to take off." The pirate didn't have to think hard about that one. He dropped what he had and ran.

John shot one of the intruders and took his sword. Then between plantation hands and John, the battle was in full form. Maria had her back to her husband, each covering the other. "Where is that brother of yours when you need him?" She stated in an irritated voice. John's arm caught the side of a blade. Not deep but Maria went hostile. "No one cuts my family!" Then she ran her blade through the man.

"Maria, this is why I don't take you out much." John was laughing. His wife was too busy to react, but she gave him a dirty look and proceeded to fight, willing herself to protect her, home, husband, and belongings. Men were in the house, removing anything they could.

John's arm was bleeding, "Let them go, we can replace all of that. Let's check on the plantation hands. They are the most important. No one will force our people into slaves on a pirate ship"

CHAPTER 3

"Uncle Jamie, where is this island that you talk about? I won't tell Mother."

Jamie smiled at his nephew. "There is a place where two oceans meet. Right in the middle of two large islands, there is a smaller volcanic island. There between the islands the ocean is fast. No one could get past the rocks between the shores. The sea flows from one ocean to the other. This place is as mysterious as it is dangerous. No one has ever come back from this small island. Above the middle Island, is a cloud of white mist, probably from the steam released from inside of the mountain, then trapped forever. Sometimes just before a big storm, the water on the north and the south of the island is almost calm. The rocks between the shores are visible, and could almost be traveled through. That is when the trouble all starts. Normally, water is much too fast to get by the island, but the calm before the storm makes everything different. This one day was just like that. The sky turned dark, then no wind, but the wind came back as strong as any that I have ever seen. The ocean turned green and white with foam, where the Atlantic Ocean flows to the Caribbean Sea, waiting for someone to experience the treachery. The sea was like a sheet of glass. Slowly the tide ebbed out. Could this be an ocean? It looked like an endless lake as far as anyone could see. At some point, before the storm hit. I could hopscotch from one island to the other, but only for a short time. The tide might drop lower and lower. I saw fish and coral that had never been seen before on the bottom of the sea. But this was the time to run, not to stop and wonder at nature's gifts; for when the tide comes back, it will come back with the fury of the devil himself. Out from the island, the ships know that this is one place that should be given a wide berth. To be caught in the flow of water from one ocean to the other would be the end for ship and crew."

This island, like so many others, has mountains in the center. But this mountain had smoke pouring out of it day after day. They call it a volcano. The jungle was so thick a man could not walk through it without a machete to clear a path. When the wind stops, and ships drift closer to the tropical sand on the beach, sailors can hear a threatening danger approaching, a scream so loud and shrill that it makes goosebumps rise on their entire bodies. Then more of the high pitch sounds of a banshee herself until the shrillness was so loud that no one could take it anymore. Sometimes a ship now gets too close to the east side of the island; by then it's too late. It will end up on the rocks, only to be crushed by the sea. Then the porter can hear the warning coming from the island. There is nothing that can be done at this point. If the sea doesn't get him, the Shee will. They say the only other thing that one hears after the Shee shipwrecked the sailors who have the misfortune of ending up on the shore is the silence of doom. That will be the end of them. You have arrived permanently at Island of the Shee."

CHAPTER 4

It was early; the aroma of the wind and flowers of the tropical island imbued the air with a Delian mystery. The road from the sugar plantation led down the side of the small mountain; back and forth the road wound until it arrived at the small town at the harbor. As the uncle and nephew walked down the rock and dirt road, they talked and laughed. Johnathan's uncle was larger than anyone else on the island and his smile was larger than that. His blue eyes complemented his smile. He reached over to put his huge hand on his nephew's shoulder.

"Uncle Jamie," said the boy. "My father would have told me if there was an island like that. Is there really a place like that?" The boy was an inquisitive soul who was almost driven to find the answers to life's questions.

"Johnathan, would you like me to stop talking about the island?"

The boy, seven years young, smiled. "No, Uncle Jamie, I want to hear more."

He looked at his uncle with intelligent blue eyes that begged for more information. The boy looked up at his uncle and smiled. His hair was bleached by the sun, he had a healthy tan and a smile that was as authentic as the island itself.

His uncle suddenly reached for his nephew, picked him up in the air, and said, "Johnathan you are the best thing that has ever happened to me. And I will always tell you the truth." And down the mountain they went, laughing all the way.

Today, Johnathan was hiking down the mountain to the harbor town. He had been there many times before with his uncle. Going down to the town was easy. But coming back, that was another thing. The road or path was traveled by many with carts full of fruits and sugar from the plantations, but rutted and bumpy. As they continued down the road, and they met someone, a smile and greeting cheered everyone on the journey. That was the way things were. Everyone was on island time. It was a truly happy place to be.

“Not a bad walk, Johnathan,” said Uncle Jamie. “Going down is the easy part. Coming back, we will see how well you do. The last time, if I remember right, I had to carry you on my shoulders. And you were fast asleep.”

Johnathan looked out over the jungle past the wild red and orange flowers that grew everywhere on the island. He could see the bay as they turned down the path. The ships were docked next to the piers. Masts towered far above their own ship and many of the buildings. The fort on the east side of the bay stood overlooking the water and protecting the town. The water was a bright dark blue. Uncle Jamie had told him that was because the water was very deep. “Uncle Jamie,” asked Johnathan, is the island out there?” Johnathan pointed out at the blue sea.

Johnathan’s Uncle answered. “Yes, and I hope that you never have to see it.” When Johnathan’s uncle was in port, they went everywhere together. Uncle Jamie was always telling Johnathan stories about the adventures of the sea. But the one that Johnathan wanted to hear the most was about the Island of the Shee. But, sometimes, Uncle Jamie would tell the boy about England. “Johnathan, can you feel the warmth of the sun? When I was about your age, like you, your father and I would play in the winter. The air was cold enough to see your breath each time you breathed. Then instead of rain, it would snow.” The boy looked up at his uncle with questioning eyes. He had never heard of snow. Johnathan’s Uncle laughed. “You will like snow. When the air becomes very cold, the rain turns into white flakes, each one different from the other. They float to the ground like feathers in the breeze. Each one on top of the other; sometimes, entire mountains are covered with the white powder.” Now Johnathan was laughing.

“What, you don’t believe me? The air gets so cold you can’t hold your teeth together. They jump up and down. The colder you get, the more your teeth chatter.”

“Uncle Jamie, I have never seen white rain.” Johnathan moved his head a little so he could see his uncle’s face; with a smile, Johnathan said, "I think I will stay right here, but tell me more about the homeland. So far it does not sound like a very good place."

"Ah, Johnathan, my boy, someday you will have to go back for school. You can't learn everything here on the island. But you can't learn everything in England either. You will have the best of both worlds. When you get there, you will see if your Uncle Jamie be telling the truth. But until that day we have the island sun and warm breeze. But look out, boy, for when the breeze stops, and the blue ocean turns a bright green with white foam on her waves, she is building up her energy for something big because there is a storm brewing. Not just any storm, a storm that will make a Christian out of any sailor."

"Uncle, why does the wind stop?"

"Johnathan, if you have a small stream of water, it does not hurt anything. But if you dam up the end and let the water rise, the small stream gets smaller and smaller till there is no more. Then you let the dam break and the more water you have stored the more damage it can do. The wind and the sea work in the same way. When you feel the sea go calm, it is time to be ready. For the sea will not give you a second chance." Johnathan shook his head and laughed. It is not that he didn't believe his uncle, but he could tell some good stories.

They were coming down to the town square. They walked past the Fort. Most of the buildings were made of limestone. Most were different shades of gray taken from the sea. "Now stay by my side Johnathan. Or you might end up as someone's cabin boy. Then I would have to tell your mother that I had misplaced you."

"Mother would not like that Uncle Jamie." laughed Johnathan.

Johnathan's uncle burst out in laughter. "No, she probably would not. I don't think I would even go back if I lost you. She would chase me right down the road back to town. So, you would be doing us both a favor if you stayed right by my side." This time he did not laugh.

"Yes, Uncle," Johnathan answered, with his head down. This time there was no smile in his voice. He sensed a quiet forbidding and almost fear-emanating from his huge friend.

As they walked down the streets to the harbor, Uncle Jamie spoke to everyone when he saw them. Then he would tell Johnathan, "Ah, I don't trust that one, or he is not so bad when he is sober." They kept walking right to the dock. Then there were the ones who could not look Uncle Jamie in the eye. "Watch the ones that can't look you in the eye, boy. They are up to no good." But all in all, everyone was busy doing something. Some were drinking. Some were working. Johnathan stayed very close to his uncle.

Just then, two men came from out of nowhere. "Are you Captain James?" One of the men asked.

"I am," replied Jamie. "Who wants to know?"

"My shipmate and I would be looking to join your crew." The two men smiled. Between them they did not have enough teeth for one man, let alone two. And the smell of the two was enough to attract any bottom dweller. Uncle Jamie stood almost a foot above the two. He smiled and answered, "The best thing you could do now is turn around and go back where you came from. I don't think you two would fit in well with my crew or ship." Jamie kept his hand on his sword.

The two men did not smile anymore. The one who seemed a little smarter than the other took off his hat and lowered one eye. "I hope that we meet again, Captain." Then they slowly moved backwards, as though they were slithering back into their cave.

"Uncle Jamie, those men scare me." he rubbed his arm to ease the goosebumps that came unbidding.

"You have every right to be scared of them. I don't know what they were after, but it was not to join my crew." They kept walking past the small marketplace, all the stores facing the bay. All the ladies smiled at the captain. Johnathan watched as his uncle returned greetings and flirted with all the women regardless of their age. They strolled down to the docks. Uncle Jamie walked over to one of the meanest-looking men Johnathan had ever laid his eyes on. Is she ready to load?" asked Uncle Jamie."

"She be ready in a few hours. The crew are already getting her ready for sea, Captain."

"I will tell my brother to have the sugar down here at daylight." Jamie held out his hand. The other man took it. Then he nodded, and made a low snarl, almost a growl, then went back to work.

Johnathan was staring right up at his uncle. "Uncle Jamie, did that man growl at you?"

Jamie just laughed. He put his arm on Johnathan's head. "Come on, boy, there is something I would like to show you." Apparently, Jamie was deflecting the boy's question, one that he did not want to answer. They walked over to the docks. The bay, with the blue ocean behind it, was where Johnathan was looking. What else was he supposed to see? "Well, what do you think boy?" asked Uncle Jamie.

Johnathan was looking out to sea, "The sea, Sir?"

"No, not the sea." Uncle Jamie was growing a little impatient. He picked up the boy and pointed to the ship that they were standing next to. "Do you know what this is?" Before Johnathan could answer, a man on the ship called down at them.

"Captain, are you coming aboard, sir?"

Captain James, answered. "We would like that," and walked on the plank to the ship. Johnathan had never been on a ship before. Everything was so clean. All the men were working. When Uncle Jamie got closer to the men, they would greet him with, "Captain." Up in the ropes, the men were humming a tune. But Johnathan could not make out what they were singing. Everyone sounded happy.

The first mate walked over to the captain. "Is this the new cabin boy you have been talking about; we have a lot of pots to be cleaned in the galley." The first mate winked at the captain. Johnathan grabbed his uncle.

"No, this be Johnathan. His father and I own this ship. He might be your captain someday."

Upon hearing this Johnathan let go of his uncle. "Me, sir?" he asked.

The first mate started laughing. "Well, pleased to meet you, Johnathan." Then he yelled to the crew. "Now hear this. This is Captain Johnathan, so treat him well." From all over the ship came the reply, "Aye, aye, sir."

"Christian," Uncle Jamie said to the first mate. "Would you be so kind as to show my nephew our ship?"

"Aye, aye, Sir," he smiled at Johnathan, "he will be in good hands."

"Johnathan, I have to go and be Captain for a little while. Try not to let Christian put you to work."

They watched the captain walk away. "Your uncle is a good man. There not be a man on the ship that would do less than give his life for him." This made Johnathan very happy as he was extremely proud of his uncle. As he watched him walk away, he suddenly realized how large his uncle was. He stood above everyone else whom he came close to. Well, Johnathan, let's take a walk," said the first mate. "You can call me Christian." Johnathan already took a liking to the first mate. He felt very secure around him. They walked over to the rails. "Look out there, Johnathan, all the people scurrying around. Some of them were working and some of them trying to get something out of someone else for nothing." Christian pointed to children playing some indescribable games. "See the children playing on the docks over there? They are just waiting for the right person to come by. Then they will be in every pocket of the unsuspecting person before he knows it. This is a busy harbor. Your father and your uncle play a large part in that."

"Christian," asked Johnathan, why do you have so many guns?"

The first mate stopped. "Sometimes the more you have, the less you have to use them. There are many pirates on the water, waiting for ships with unsuspecting crews, and they don't care about anyone except themselves. Honest is not in their vocabulary. This ship can outsail and outgun about any other ship on the sea. And your uncle is the right captain for her. No pirate in his right mind would attack this ship. Judge a captain by his ship and crew. Look how clean the ship is. The crew takes pride in caring for her because she is like a strong and beautiful woman." They spent the time waiting for Uncle Jamie to get through with whatever he had to do. Little by little all of the crew started to gather around the boy. Then they started to tell him stories, many about his uncle. One of the crew asked Johnathan, "What do you know of the sea? Have you heard of some of the places we have been with your uncle?"

Johnathan was all ears. Then he asked, "Have you ever seen the Island of the Shee?" No one answered. The seagulls begging for food was the only sound.

Christian took Johnathan aside. "Aye, we have heard of that place and some of us have been there. May we never see it again; let us not speak of it."

The lad nodded his head. "Yes sir." The timing was perfect. The first mate pointed to Captain James returning.

"It looks like I should take my nephew off the ship so you swabs can get back to work. We sail in two days." Jamie and the crew were smiling, as they started off the ship, Johnathan waved to the crew, and they returned the favor.

"You made a good showing for the crew, Johnathan. They would do anything for you. You have made friends for life."

"I like them all, Uncle Jamie."

As they walked down the plank to the dock, the two men who stopped them earlier were looking at the ship. When they saw the captain, they started to slink away. Jamie called back to the ship. "Christian,"

"Aye Captain."

"See to it that these two are removed from the dock. And that they never get that close to the ship again." The first mate ordered four men down on the dock at once. The two men were already running for their lives.

"We won't be seeing them again; I wonder what they were up to." Jamie put Johnathan on his back, and off they went back up the mountain. When they were at the base of the mountain Jamie stopped and turned. "Now what do you see, boy?"

Johnathan answered, "The best ship and crew on the sea."

Uncle Jamie watched Johnathan from the corner of his eye. "Ah, I think that I might be in love with my ship. I could watch her all day."

"Uncle Jamie, you can't be in love with a ship," Johnathan was giggling."

"Sure, you can. You can love the ship, the sea, or a woman. They can all give you a lot of trouble or love. Now don't you tell your mother I said that; that is an order."

"Aye, aye, Captain," Johnathan answered.

"Look at the tallest mast on the ship. See that flag, it is your father's flag. When you see that blue flag with a dove holding a cannon, you know that your Uncle Jamie is near." The name of the ship is The Fighting Dove. "Uncle Jamie, you told Christian that you are going to sea in two days."

"That is right," said Uncle Jamie.

"How long will you be gone?" Johnathan was starting to get teary-eyed.

Uncle Jamie could see that Johnathan was starting to get upset. "It is a long trip. If the wind treats us right, I will be back in no time at all. Besides, your father and mother need supplies for the plantation. And I need to take the sugar to market."

"Can I go with you, Uncle Jamie?" Disappointment was obvious by the drop in his shoulders.

"Not this trip. But the way you are growing, it won't be long. And the crew would like you to be with them. Now, boy, are you walking or riding?" "I'm riding," said Johnathan. And he gave his uncle a bear hug.

When they met some of the ladies walking on the road, they would giggle and say hello to the captain. It was like that in the harbor town as well. Jamie would greet them with, "Good afternoon ladies." Then he would act like he had a hat on and tip it. That made Johnathan giggle. Uncle Jamie would reach up and tickle Johnathan until he stopped laughing. And they were laughing all the way up the mountain until they were out of sight. The road back was a long one. It was easy going down but took forever going back. Johnathan had never seen the entire island. They could have gone by horseback. But Uncle Jamie liked to go slow and enjoy the walk. Uncle Jamie always said,

"There will be plenty of times when you have to go fast. So, enjoy life when you can." These were the best of times, a boy and his uncle. Neither one could ask for anything more. Away they went up the dirt road, jungle on both sides.

"Now, Johnathan, you stay on the road. You would not last long in the jungle. There are things in the jungle that even I don't know about."

"Yes, sir," came the reply, Johnathan was happy to stay on his uncle's shoulders, where he knew he was safe.

The road was busy, islanders walking, some with carts, but as they say in the islands, everyone is on island time. No one appeared to be in a hurry. "Johnathan, these are good people. They may be on island time, but they are there when you need them. Do not ever think we are better than they are." Would you like me to tell you a story boy?"

What an easy question. "Yes, Uncle Jamie. Is it about the island that I'm not supposed to talk about?"

"Yes boy. We would not want your mother to know that I was telling you scary stories, right?"

Johnathan knew only too well, that his mother would not like the stories of the sea from Uncle Jamie. "I won't tell her, Uncle Jamie. Please tell me more about the island." Johnathan pleaded with his uncle.

"All right, I will tell you." And the story began.

"A few years ago, my crew and I were coming back from the homeland. The first part of the trip was a sailor's dream. Good seas, wind, and no pirates. I have never seen the ocean so blue. Like a picture, it was. I should have known it would never last. Then the wind stopped. We drifted for days. We were at the mercy of the sea. She took us where she wanted. There was nothing anyone could do. The air was hot. My clothes clung to my back. This was the calm before the storm."

Johnathan did not say a word. He was afraid that he would miss something. Uncle Jamie continued. "The blue sea turned as smooth as glass. At the same time, the water turned green. Not any kind of green, mind you, a green that glowed. Still no wind, we were at the mercy of the sea. Then I could see them. Three islands, the one to the north, was long. The one from the South was also long. I could not see the end of either of them. Then the one in the center was so close to the other two. You could see the jagged rocks linking all three islands. There was an ominous white cloud that hung over the island. All day we drifted closer and closer to the island between the other two. Then, you could hear the little island. It started to scream, the sound from the island was like nothing I had ever heard before. A cold chill went down the back of every man of the crew. The closer we came, the louder the screams resounded. Not a cloud in the sky, except for the one over the island. It seemed to be turning into itself, never leaving the island. Up in the sky coming in and out of the sky were two flying reptiles. One of them would breathe fire, or so it looked like. The other one did not. Each time the larger one would breathe fire he would drop in the air, after three times he landed on the island."

Johnathan was fixed on every word. He watched his uncle talk as if he was reliving the day again. His eyes grew round and big as he envisioned the clouded island emerging.

"The other reptile floated along instantaneously. He shot off like a shooting star back into the cloud. We never saw them again. The beach was in sight. We could see the trees moving, but nothing came out. Just when we were close enough to swim to shore, the sails filled with wind. I turned the ship to port. The screams were so loud that the crew could not hear a word that I said. They did not have to. They knew what to do." Uncle Jamie was sweating. He looked at Johnathan, and Jamie realized he was scaring the boy. "I guess I got carried away, boy."

"What happened then, Uncle?" Johnathan was begging for more.

"Well now, they call that the Island of the Shee. With the wind picking up we sailed south for home, but not before the sea became angry. Now we were at the mercy of the storm. She was a rough storm. But the crew thought it was nothing compared to what the island would have done to us. To this day I think the island is haunted. The storm was a bad one. But if not for the storm, we would not have made it."

Uncle Jamie turned and looked at Johnathan. "We might not tell your mother about the stories of the island."

Johnathan shook his head, "I think that would be a good idea. Mother would not like this story."

"You are probably right. I won't tell her if you don't," said Uncle Jamie.

The two walked for a while. Uncle Jamie started talking again. As if he was recalling a bad dream. "If you are on the east side of the Island on a good day, the waves flow past the island, over the rocks so fast that no one could make it to the island. Sailors would end up on the rocks in a very bad way. But enough about the sea and the islands, what do you think your mother will feed us tonight?" Uncle Jamie knew he had scared the boy. So, he tried to change the talk to something else. It did not work.

"Uncle Jamie, does anyone live on the other islands?" asked Johnathan.

"They, say, on the island to the north, cannibals. And the one to the south, pirates."

"What are cannibals, Uncle Jamie?"

"A tribe of people who eat other people," Jamie answered. With no additional information though he didn't want to think about that practice.

"Do you think the pirates go to the small island in the middle?" asked Johnathan."

"Maybe, but I doubt it. No one really knows if the pirates are there. It would be the perfect place for them. No one would go there trying to find them. It would be a good place to stay away from."

"You really have been to the Island of the Shee?" asked Johnathan.

Uncle Jamie stopped. "Let us sit for a spell. We are almost home. You won't say a word to your mother, will you?" He looked Johnathan right in the eyes. Then he smiled. "I would like to have my dinner tonight."

Johnathan stood up and pushed his chest out. "I will not say a word, Captain."

"Well, then the answer is yes. And I hope that I never see it again."

Johnathan kept talking. What is a Shee?"

"Best as I can tell, it is short for banshee. One of the crew said he had heard that scream before in his homeland when he was just a lad in Ireland. For me, I don't know. The sound was more like a scream and a cry at the same time. It sent a chill up and down the backbone of every man in the crew. I have never heard anything like it."

"What happened to your ship?"

"The ship, bless her, held her own. We were close enough to see the fruit in the palm trees. The sea was calm going past the island. Then it flowed like the mightiest river rapids between the islands. We were headed right for the small island. Then by the grace of God, the wind filled our sails, not a minute too soon. I already had the rudder on course to port. I was waiting for the crash of the rocks on the hull. But it was not to be. The storm came out of nowhere and put us back on course. We rode out the storm for half a day. At times I thought our mast would break. We were blown south from our route. But as soon as the storm let up, we made it back to port. I lost one man, the one who said that he had heard the screams before. God rest his soul. I can still hear his screams as the waves took him to the shore. The island of the devil itself, it was. With the storm, we did not have the option of trying to save the man. The storm took us right out to the sea. The storm, as bad as it was, saved us from the island."

Suddenly Uncle Jamie stood up. "Do you hear that gunfire; it is coming from the plantation."

"Uncle Jamie, someone is running down the road."

"Johnathan, is that one of your father's people? Something must be wrong. Be very quiet and do what I say. Get down, and hide off the road in the jungle," whispered Jamie.

Johnathan knew this was not a good thing. Uncle Jamie would never ask him to get off the road, let alone to hide in the jungle unless there was real danger. They waited. Johnathan's heart was pounding. Surely everyone could hear his heart. He remembered about the jungle and took a look about. He could see birds in the trees, bugs moving on the ground and a funny-looking animal looking right at him. One eye going one way, and the other still. Then it jumped for Johnathan, going right over his head. Johnathan tried to scream, but Uncle Jamie quickly put his hand over Johnathan's mouth.

Johnathan quickly turned toward his uncle. He had his finger over his lips. Johnathan knew to be quiet, forgetting about the lizard jumping over him. He watched his uncle make ready to spring.

First, the Captain's powerful arm sprang out and caught the man right in the mid-section, stopping him at once.

The man was running for his life. He was a young black man from the plantation.

"Where might you be going in such a hurry," asked Uncle Jamie?

"Captain," said the man. "Pirates, they must have come through the jungle."

"Are they at the plantation? How many are there? Did they get into the main house?" The man did not know. Johnathan had never seen his uncle that mad. Jamie held the man. "Do you know who Johnathan is?"

"Yes, Captain," he stuttered in terror.

"Your new job is to keep a good eye on Johnathan, do you understand me?" "Yes, Captain, I will watch."

"If anything happens to him, you will wish the pirates had got you," yelled Jamie.

Jamie could see that he was scaring Johnathan and the black man. In a much calmer voice, he looked right at the two. "Johnathan, I am going ahead. You and your new friend come behind me. Hide in the mill until it is quiet. Then I will come and get you."

Johnathan did not miss a word. "Yes Uncle, we will be there." He spoke in a very small voice; he was almost panicked.

"Johnathan," said Uncle Jamie. "Your new friend is more scared than you are. I love you Johnathan, and I will be back to get you."

Uncle Jamie looked at the black man, who must have been at least twenty-five years old. He grabbed the man's right hand. "You take care of my nephew. Thank you."

The man nodded his head. Not daring to argue with the big man.

Then Uncle Jamie was gone.

Johnathan took the black man's hand. He remembered what his uncle had said. "Take your time; there will be plenty of time later to run." They started up the mountain slowly. As they headed for the plantation, neither one of them said a word.

Ahead of them, Captain Jamie could see the plantation. He could hear people yelling. He pulled his pistol and sword. He ran toward the smoke.

Johnathan and his new friend were now running up the road. They were as quiet as they could manage. They also could hear the shouting and see the smoke. The mill was just ahead. They ran for it and ducked inside. They both sat in the shadows of the dirt floor, holding hands. "Can you talk?" asked Johnathan.

The man nodded his head yes, "But not now."

Johnathan thought that was probably a good thing. Everything was going so fast. They were both very tired, but they did not think about it. Johnathan remembered what his uncle had said, "There will be plenty of time to rush later." For now, wait till Uncle Jamie comes. The smell of the dirt and stone floor would forever be in Johnathan's dreams. He started to close his eyes. Johnathan was caught in a moment of thought. "I am tired. How long will we be there? When will Uncle Jamie come? I have never been in the mill before. I have heard father talking about it. How could I think of all these questions at once?"

The black man grabbed Johnathan's arm. Johnathan could feel him shake. The calm quietness was broken by laughter coming down the road. Johnathan could feel the sweat running down the arm of his new friend. The black man pointed at his leg. There on his knee was a scorpion. The black spider was hard to see. Then it turned and jumped to the ground. The black man had to put his own hand over his mouth to keep his sanity. The voices were just outside of the mill.

Johnathan had never heard them before. "They must be the pirates," he thought. Johnathan was watching the scorpion. It had landed in front of the man's bare feet. Johnathan watched in horror as the black man shook. The pirates strutted past the mill, still laughing. They had not seen the two. Nor had the two seen them. Johnathan was trying not to cry. Uncle Jamie would be disappointed in him if he did, but he was terrified – mother, his father, Uncle Jamie, where are they?

Then without warning the small but lethal creature turned back, confronting the man. He panicked and tried to kick the scorpion away. This turned out to be a very bad response, which he and Johnathan soon found out. Then the scream; Johnathan thought the man was going to squeeze his hand off. "He must be in great pain; Johnathan had never heard anything like this agony before. Where did this small but deadly thing go? It moved faster than anything Johnathan had ever seen in his entire life of seven years. Johnathan could not speak for the clattering of his teeth and the closing of his throat. The road that had been full of the sounds of the jungle and the laughter of the pirates was now a different kind of noise, or the lack of it. The only thing Johnathan could hear was what was caused by the pain of the scorpion to the man next to him. Nothing was left to do. Which was good because they were too scared to move, even if they had to. Johnathan and his friend sat and waited. The moments seemed like hours. Both of them were sweating now with fear. A fear that Johnathan had never felt before was upon him. He could not look at his friend; his head would not turn, no matter how he tried. The mill was suddenly colder now than ever before. All they could see was light under the door, then darkness. They did not have to wait very long. The door smashed open. The force of the door opening left it hanging by one hinge. There was silence, the sunlight rushed in. What little they could see was now impossible with the sudden flow of light that had overtaken the mill. The two put their hands over their eyes to shield them from the rush of sunlight. The first thing Johnathan could see was the scorpion. The scorpion ran toward the light for the jungle, right between the legs of the pirate. Another man right behind him crushed him with his boot. Slowly they stared at the pirate's boots. Johnathan stopped when he saw the blade of the sword, still dripping blood.

"Well, look what we have here, a slave and a cabin boy."

All Johnathan could think about was his family and wondered whose blood it was. He found a stone, just the right size to take down the pirate. Johnathan pushed off the hand of his friend. With his left hand full of dirt and the right with the stone, he stood up to fight. Adrenaline had given him the strength of ten boys. The first hand let go of the dirt, right in the face of the pirate with the sword. Johnathan only wished that he could throw the scorpion that had given them away. With the second hand, he hit the pirate in the face with his rock. The pirate screamed as he went to his knees.

Johnathan yelled, "Get up and run. Run as fast as you can." They, he and his nameless friend, ran out of the mill past the pirate. Johnathan was first. He headed for the jungle. Just before he disappeared in the leaves of the jungle, Johnathan heard a shot of a pistol, then a moan.

Johnathan could not move. He froze with fear. His arms were in the air, ready for the jump into the jungle and freedom. But freedom was not to be this day.

Johnathan turned slowly. His friend with no name lay face down in the dirt. Johnathan ran to him. He bent down, only to be snatched by rough hands and the only thing he saw was a fist to his face, then nothing, darkness the abyss.

CHAPTER 5

Jamie soon arrived at the plantation. His mind was on his nephew, but he also knew that his brother and wife needed his help. With lightning speed, he went into gear. He saw a fire at the main house. The servants had it almost under control.

As far as he could see, the pirates had stormed the plantation and taken anything that they could carry. He could see his brother at the house fighting three of the scoundrels; they did not have a chance. Then he heard the scream, "Jamie," it was his sister-in-law. Her dress was torn. She was holding off one pirate on her own, but slowly losing the battle. Jamie was on him with the speed of a cat. The man never saw him coming. "I think she might want to stay a little longer," he told the pirate as he ran him through with his sword. He nodded to his brother's wife and acted as if he tipped his hat, even though he never had one, then went for the next pirate, then the next. Soon the outlaws were running. All of the pirates headed for the jungle, except two. They went down the road that Jamie had come from.

Johnathan's father was at the house, his arm covered with blood. He showed no signs of slowing down. He was giving orders for the servants to put out the fires.

Jamie helped his sister-in-law regain her balance, "Are you all right Maria?" he asked.

She was shaken, but all right. "Where is Johnathan?" she screamed.

"He is hiding in the mill with one of the servants. If you are all right, I will go and get him."

"I'm coming with you," she said. Maria ripped off part of her dress so she could ride in her petticoat.

There were two horses near the house calmly eating their oats and hay; Jamie and his sister-in-law jumped on them and were off down the hill before the animals had time to panic.

As they passed the house, Maria screamed to her husband. "We are going to rescue Johnathan." He acknowledged her with a short wave of his arm and continued to put out the fire started by the pirates.

Darkness was coming as they approached the mill. Jamie was off the horse before it had stopped. The young black man lay in the road. Jamie raised him up. "Captain," he said. "They took your nephew," he said in a low voice; then he collapsed.

"Jamie," cried Maria.

The captain lowered the man's head gently to the ground. The young man was about to close his eyes, when he raised his hand, and put it on Jamie's hand. "Maria, take this man back to the house. He is a good man; take care of him. Jamie wanted Marie to be at her home safely if things got ugly here; he would miss having her at his back, but no other reasonable choice existed. Jamie stood and looked around. He saw Johnathan's white shirt. It was ripped and dirty. He quickly picked it up. "Maria, when you see this shirt under my flag, you will know Johnathan is all right. Now I must go, I have a boy to find."

All that Maria could see was a six-foot five shadow of her brother-in- law moving with the wind. His arms filled out the sleeves of his shirt. For a man of his size, he was agile and fast. Up until this time, he had never raised his voice in anger, even when he gave an order. He did not have to. Not out of fear, but respect. Maybe this time, things would be different.

CHAPTER 6

Johnathan opened one eye. In the daylight, he could smell the salty air of the sea. He tried to open the other eye, but it was swollen shut. Instinctively, he put his hand over his eye. He had never felt pain like this before. He started to cry, but quickly thought of his uncle. "Uncle Jamie would not cry, so I won't either." Johnathan tried not to move as he looked around as he did not want to attract any attention. He was lying on a coil of rope on the deck of a ship. A ship much too dirty to be his uncle's. The rope was next to a mast. "What is that smell?" he thought. It was not long before the mystery of the odor unfolded.

Johnathan stared up at the shadow in the sun. It was a man laughing at him. "Here you little squid. Put this on your eye. It will make it feel better." The man threw a wet rag to the scared boy who couldn't decide which odor was worse-the filthy man or filthy the rag.

"The captain would like to see you if you don't mind." He raised Johnathan by the hair, and then dragged the kicking boy over the deck, laughing all the way.

"That will be enough of that, Wink." The pirate let go of the boy. "Stand up, boy."

Johnathan stood facing the man. His face was deeply scarred, especially over and under his left eye, and his lip was cut just enough for two of his teeth to show. He wore a dark hat that covered his black hair. But his clothes were better than anyone else's that he could see.

"Now who would you be," asked the man.

"My name is Johnathan," he said as he sidled quietly away from his dirty rag man. "Johnathan, I am the captain. You are on my ship. While you are my ship, you will give the crew respect. Or maybe you would like to swim back to your island?"

“Your crewman is dirty, and he smells,” answered Johnathan pointing at Wink.

Wink pulled his dagger. “Let me slit his throat?”

“Ah, Johnathan, that not be the way to talk to Wink. Ye see, he does not particularly like you. Seeing how you knocked out his teeth with a rock.”

Now the boy remembered the man “My uncle will come and get me. And he does not like pirates,” exclaimed Johnathan, more bravely than he felt.

“Who might your uncle be Johnathan,” asked the captain.

“Johnathan answered, “Captain Jamie James.”

There was a pause, then “Let me throw him over the rail, Captain. We don’t want James coming after us,” pleaded Wink.

The captain scratched his beard. Then he stared right into the eyes of Wink. “If this boy truly is James’ nephew, we will need him later. Wink, go about ye duties. Let me talk to the lad.” The pirate left, making a growling noise; and as he walked away, he spit right near Johnathan’s feet.

Johnathan could see the newly found stress that was now laid upon the captain was obvious. He walked over and sat down on a barrel next to Johnathan. He sat there watching Johnathan for a while. Then he asked, “Does your eye hurt much?” The pirate captain scratched his beard.

Johnathan nodded yes.

“Let me have a look at it.” The captain reached over and pulled down the wet rag Johnathan was holding. “Woo, that is a real nasty eye. Come into my cabin so I can have a better look at it.”

Johnathan followed the captain indecisively. When they entered his cabin, Johnathan saw items that belonged to his mother and father. There was also treasure that he had not seen before, but he was sure that all the booty was valuable. The captain was watching the boy as his eyes wandered over the contents of the room, but Johnathan was aware of the pirate’s eyes following his own.

"Now let me see that eye of yours." The captain put Johnathan in one of his chairs around the table. He opened a cabinet and took out a bottle. He approached the boy with a smile. "Hold still, this might hurt some." Johnathan let the man dress his wounds. He barely jerked, even though the pain was considerable. The captain put a clean patch over Johnathan's eye. "You look like one of us, lad."

In a quiet but stern voice, Johnathan answered, "I will never look like one of you." He was relieved that his voice did not shake when he said that. The captain was quick to answer. "Ah, ye never know, you might come to like me. Now Wink, that might be a little bit harder."

Johnathan answered, "Wink smells like a foul pig."

The captain laughed, "He does that indeed." the captain went over to one of the chests and opened it. He pulled out a shirt. "It's a little big, but it will look right smart on you." As he was putting the shirt on, Johnathan was eyeing some fruit on the captain's table. "Help yourself, lad, then go topside and meet the crew. But try to stay away from Wink."

"Why do you call him Wink?" Johnathan asked while holding his eye.

The captain smiled. But he did not let the boy see it. He turned, "It is short for Stink. But Wink gets rather upset when we call him Stink." Johnathan almost smiled.

"Take some fruit. Then go top side and stay clear of Wink. Do you understand?"

"Yes, Sir," Johnathan answered from the force of habit.

Johnathan climbed up and out to the deck. He watched the crew watch him. The ship smelled and was quite dirty. There were cannons everywhere. But very few of them were the same. The sails were sewn in many places.

Some had holes and some were ripped. There were two men up in the sails repairing the new holes. As Johnathan was standing next to the rail looking out to sea, he was approached by yet another member of the crew. Johnathan had not seen this one before. At least he did not smell.

"So, you be the new cabin boy. Kind of meek, aren't you? The captain asked me to keep an eye on you. Mind you, I don't very much like children. They take up space and eat food that the rest of us need." Johnathan listened to the pirate, but the entire time he was thinking of his uncle. "These men would not be acting so brave if Uncle Jamie were here."

"Do you hear me squid, "Growled the pirate. When Johnathan did not answer, the smelly pirate picked him up and started to shake him. "Did you hear me squid?"

"You won't treat me like that when my uncle gets here," replied Johnathan. This made the pirate more than angry. The pirate raised his hand to hit the boy. Johnathan braced for the blow. He opened his eye. The captain was there, holding the arm of the pirate. The leader spoke quietly but firmly to Wink.

"This boy is a guest on my ship. I would suggest that you honor my word. I would not take it kindly if the young man was hurt more than he already is. This little Squid, as you call him, is my guest. We would not want anything to happen to Uncle Jamie's nephew now, would we, Mr. Jon?" Mr. Jon gently lowered Johnathan to the deck. As soon as he let go, Johnathan pulled back from him, but he knew better than to say anything right then. Mr. Jon had a surprised look also. The captain had never corrected him before.

The captain turned to Johnathan. "I told you I would look after you, lad. Now go about and look around." The captain walked over to the first mate. He put his arm around the first mate. "Jon, don't disappoint me. The lad is worth far more alive and well than hurt or dead. If I know his uncle, he is on his way right now to fetch him. Take care of him for me, won't you?"

Then the captain put pressure on the first mate's neck until fear showed in his face. Jon quickly assured. Mr. Jon knew that the captain could easily snap his neck. The pirate captain wasn't easy to look at when he was normal. But when he was disturbed about something, his face went from bad to scary. When he stared at the first mate, Mr. Jon almost wet his pants. Johnathan was still standing right where he stopped. The captain walked over to him. Johnathan had never before seen the true face of the pirate captain; otherwise, he probably would have run for his life. “Again, I apologize for that misunderstanding. I asked Mr. Jon to look after you. He thought you might be our new cabin boy. I would be much surprised if he makes a mistake again. But be careful, lad, some of the crew would rather throw you over the side at night if they thought they could get away with it. Mr. Jon is also our navigator. He is a right and proper man.”

Johnathan answered, “Yes, sir.” The boy had enough sense not to backtalk the captain. Some of life’s lessons are learned early.

Captain LeDuval, motioned to the first mate. Jon walked over to him. The captain nodded over to the port side where a large dog was sleeping. “Don’t let the Squid get too close to that springy sea dog. I don’t think he would know the difference between his next meal and our guest.”

The first mate smiled, “Aye, Captain.” They both looked at the two hundred pounds of a sleeping mass of a dog, or half a dog and half the good lord only knows. He lay sleeping in the shade of the forecastle; neither had seen a dog like him before. But what Johnathan did not know was the beast could catch any mouse or rat then eat it. No one could get too close to him. They just let him do his job. Some time ago, they had a run in with a ship headed for the tropics. The pirates attacked the ship, and it began to sink. As they were looting the ship before they sank her, and everyone on it, the dog came aboard and has been there ever since. It was an Irish wolfhound, but the crew could not know that.

Johnathan watched the crew stow bundles and chests down below. They were in too big of a hurry to get out of port to do it before now. Johnathan turned to the sea. This time tears came down his face. He quickly wiped them away with the sleeve of his newly found shirt. He had rolled the sleeves up as far as he could. At least now he could see his hands.

“Where are you Uncle Jamie?

CHAPTER 7

The sun had set on the tropic island. But the full moon was glowing in the indigo sky. As Captain James steered his horse down the treacherous winding road to the harbor town, he could hear the drumming sound of cannons at the harbor. The noise drowned out the droning evening bugs that usually accompanied the dock. Normally, the harbor town was sleepy after sunset. But tonight, soldiers from the fort were going through the streets. The town was bright with lights. A panic was upon it. The noise drowned out the evening bugs that usually accompany the dark. Captain Jamie James rode down the last length of the windy and gloomy road. The fort was in sight. He went for the gate, which was now closed. Mountains on the other three sides, the three-story fort of brick and stone rose over the harbor and the ships, one floor beneath the surface, two above the ground and cannons on the deck above. Its mighty cannons would make any pirate ship think before attacking the well-fortified town. The governor's office was also in the fort. The main entrance to the fort consisted of large double doors spliced together. They were made of thick wood and iron, arched at the top, but not tall enough for a rider to enter on his horse, via a sitting position.

When Captain James was seen approaching the fort, he could hear someone shout, "Open the gates!" When he saw that the gates were open, he leaned over the side of the horse and was in. "They should have made that thing taller," he thought as he felt the top of the entrance rub his back. Only to be greeted by the governor himself, Jamie regained a dignified position. Jamie quickly dismounted. One of the soldiers took the horse before Jamie was off his mount. The atmosphere in the fort was tense.

"Governor, would you send someone to my ship? Tell them we are making sail with the tide."

The governor pointed to one of the soldiers. "Go to his ship." The soldier was on his mount and off.

"Did the pirates hit the town?" asked Jamie?

"No," replied the Governor. "How did you fair?"

"They attacked the plantation. They took my nephew. Do you have any idea where they came from?" asked Jamie.

"Captain, will you follow me?" asked the governor. They walked into the chart room. Five men had charts out on the tables. One spoke.

"We think they came from the north side of the island. They must have walked up the mountain through the jungle. There is a small bay they could have anchored in.

"They took Captain James's nephew," announced the governor, concerningly.

As Jamie looked over the charts, he said, "Then they did not have to wait for the tide. But where did they go? Do you have any idea?"

"Not yet, but we were about to find out. Would you like to join us?" The governor motioned for Jamie to follow, which he did.

One of the other men in the chart room said, "I would not want to be the captain of the ship that took his nephew." The others agreed.

Across the courtyard to a cell overlooking the harbor two men were inside. The soldier unlocked the cell door. Jamie and the guard walked in, the governor right behind. The small cell was not big enough to cage rats, let alone people. The two sat on a bench chained to the wall. The men could not move around the cell. Because of the small size and the fact that the rats considered the two smelly people usurpers of this space, the rats let the two pirates understand their disgust of the situation.

One of the men looked stronger and smarter than the other. Jamie went to him first. He told the other to watch closely.

"I would like to talk to this one first; release him," demanded Jamie. The Governor nodded his permission to the soldier who quickly released the man.

Jamie looked down on the man. "Where has your ship sailed to?"

The pirate did not move, but thinking he had the upper hand, taunted Jamie.

"Now why would you want to know that?"

"My nephew is on that ship." Jamie was trying to keep his voice down. "The captain said he was looking for a new cabin boy," said the prisoner with a half grin. Jamie noticed before he had walked into the cell that there was a wood pole about six feet up on the wall where the cell keys were. The post was loose and would slide in without much effort. Jamie reached down and picked up the man. He lifted him off his feet. "Governor, what is the penalty for this pirate?"

"Death by hanging."

"You cannot do anything to me as bad my captain would," said the pirate. "Go talk to the sea, you will have a better chance to find your boy." The pirate's eyes opened wide as Jamie started to walk him out of the cell. Jamie turned to the other pirate, "You're next." He watched as Jamie took the pirate. "Where did they take my nephew? this is your last chance." Before the pirate could answer Jamie picked him up and slammed him onto the wooden dowel. The stake impaled the man to the wall. Still alive, the pirate struggled. His feet didn't touch the ground again. Jamie walked back into the cell. Everyone standing there was shocked, the Governor included. Jamie turned to the other pirate who was now standing.

"Now, captain," said the governor in a calm voice, "If you kill this one also, you won't have anyone to talk to. Jamie took a step toward the pirate.

The man was now talking. "I'll talk, but you can't tell where you got it from."

Jamie picked the man up. He looked him right into his eyes. "Where have they taken my nephew? Or do you want to end up like your friend? Who, by the way, was still shaking on the wall?"

The pirate's eyes watched his friend shaking. He was still breathing, but not for long. "I cannot read the charts," he said.

You could see the anger in Jamie's face as his grip tightened around the man. He still had the pirate in the air, but dangling like his friend as though they had danced together before. "I swear to the almighty, your feet will never touch the ground if you-.

Jamie did not have time to finish. The pirate said, "You did not give me time to finish. The captain has your nephew."

"What captain?" Yelled Jamie.

The governor looked at the pirate. "I don't think I can hold the captain much longer. You might want to tell him."

Jamie squeezed the pirate who yelled in pain. "LeDuval, the Devil Captain. The island, next to the Shee."

"The island to the north or to the south?" Jamie demanded.

"To the south," whimpered the pirate. Jamie let the man drop to the floor. You could smell the fear in the man. He knew Jamie would do him in.

The governor looked at the man on the floor. Then he turned to Jamie, "There is no such place."

Jamie did not answer the governor, "Where do you anchor, what side," Jamie demanded.

The pirate was still whimpering, "There is only one side. I will have to show you." The pirate looked up smiling as if he had an edge.

"Dead men make poor navigators. You just tell me everything you know, and maybe the governor will not hang you until I get back."

"That sounds fair," said the governor. He then motioned for the soldiers to get the man on the wall.

Jamie yelled at the man, "The side of the island where the sun sets."

"Yes, the pirate answered."

While they were leaving the cell, Jamie took one last look at the pirate. "If you lied to me, you will be the next one on the wall.

The pirate watched as the soldiers pulled the unconscious pirate down from the wall. He started to move. The post on the wall pushed in just enough to hold a man was still showing. "I thought Captain James had killed you," he said.

"You didn't tell him anything did you?"

It was quiet in the cell as Jamie walked back across the yard, "Jamie, there is no Island of the Shee. It is superstition," said the governor.

Jamie stopped, "I have seen it. My crew and I were there once. I swore I would never go back. Let's get the charts out again."

"If anyone else had told me the island was real, I would not have believed them," the governor replied.

As they walked back over the yard into the chart room, the candlelight was burning bright. They walked through the open door. The three officers stared at Jamie as he entered the room. The night air was damp. "It will be light soon." Jamie could smell the sweet morning air and the luxurious scent of flowers of the tropical island.

"We must hurry. It's almost high tide." Jamie pulled out one chart, then another. He unrolled them with one of his massive fingers he dropped it down one of the maps. "Here is where the island is, right between these two islands."

"But captain, there is no island on the map," said one of the officers.

"It is there, where the two oceans meet. There is a cloud from the volcano that hides the danger. Like a serpent in the grass, it waits for its next victim." Jamie continued, "The island to the south was rumored to be inhabited by pirates; the one to the north cannibals, or head hunters. Of the three islands, only the one in the center is volcanic. Not a good place to be for any sailor, but for a pirate, maybe not so bad. May I have this map," asked Jamie?

"The fleet will be here any day; can't you wait," pleaded the Governor? He knew even before he was done asking that it was in vain. After a moment, he gave in. "Take the chart, and may God be with you," answered the Governor.

Jamie walked outside. There were two horses; the one that Jamie rode in on and another.

A soldier announced, "I will bring your mount back, captain, and see that he gets back to your brother." They walked the horses out of the fort. As they looked down at the bay, they could see the ship. Every lantern on the ship was lit. You could hear shouting on her decks. The tide was in and the wind had started to pick up. With no time to spare, the two were off. By this time, the moon was out and the town was easily seen. As they closed on the ship, Jamie could see his flag flying. The deck was a hustle of organized frenzy.

Christian yelled, "Captain, we are ready to set sail."

"Very good, Christian," Jamie yelled back. Then he turned to the soldier, "Thank you." Jamie jumped off his horse. The soldier grabbed the rein from Jamie. He did not say anything, but gave Jamie a salute. Then he watched as Jamie boarded the ship. The plank was raised as soon as the captain was on board; all the lines were pulled in and the ship was off.

Most of the time when The Fighting Dove was getting ready to put to sea it was a happy time for all. This time it was all business. The ship was brought about and all the sails were starting to fill with the wind. In just a few minutes they were out of the harbor and headed east across the deep blue ocean. On top of the mountain overlooking the east side of the island, Johnathan's mother and father watched as the ship went by, Johnathan's father with one arm in a sling, holding his wife with the other.

Maria warned, "Please, be careful Jamie!"

"Maria, my brother will be back. He will not stop until Johnathan is with him."

They watched sorrowfully, but sorrow tinged with hope as the ship sailed out of sight piercing the morning light.

CHAPTER 8

Two days into the voyage, the young boy was getting a feel for the pirate ship. His eye was much better. He could see more things, clearly almost every hour now. Johnathan was given a meal twice a day. Most of the time he could not bring himself to eat the cheese and meat for the ants and bugs, but the fruit was not bad. Mr. Jon was coming with a new plate of food for him. “Squid, don’t let me catch you throwing this overboard. I watched you pitch your meal last night. If you, do it again, I might pitch you,” warned Mr. Jon.

Johnathan took the plate from Mr. Jon. He sat on some rope coiled next to the mast, watching Mr. Jon as he walked away grumbling. Johnathan had not seen the captain since the first day, and no one else would have anything to do with him. Mr. Jon was the only one who talked to him. And that was only because the captain told him to. Johnathan went up to the aft deck next to the helm. He could see better and as no one cared what he did, so he had made up his mind that if he saw land of any kind, he would jump ship and swim for it. Now, for the first time, he could see land. They were close enough to see the trees and the pure white sand. He looked around to see if anyone was watching him, He walked down the steps to the main deck. He would wait until no one was watching, then run as fast as he could, jump over the side, and swim to the land. He waited and waited. The crew was finally occupied with throwing some garbage over the side. They were laughing and talking with one another loudly and crudely.

“This is my chance,” thought Johnathan. He looked around, then jumped to his feet and ran for the rail. Almost there, he jumped and was over the side- only to be caught by the arm and quickly hauled back aboard.

“Now that be a close one,” said the captain as he let Johnathan go on the deck. The captain smiled, “I thought you was going over the side, I did.” The captain put Johnathan down close to the large sleeping dog.

"Now a word to the wise, don't wake the sleeping dog or whatever it is. He doesn't like too many people." This awakened the brute. When Johnathan stared at the dog, the animal showed his teeth and let go with a low, powerful growl. "That is what I mean," said the captain. Now let's take a walk. There is something that you might find interesting." There was a crew member; eating a slab of meat while sitting on a stool next to the mast, the captain grabbed the food from the man.

"Captain," yelled the surprised man.

The captain smiled at Johnathan, "He really did not want this. He is too fat. We just use him for ballast. Sometimes I think that he eats too good. Would you like some?" he asked Johnathan. Johnathan eyed the meat. It looked like it had small bugs on it. He shook his head no. The captain brushed the meat off and took a bite. "Not bad, are ye sure?" Johnathan again said no. "Very well," said the captain. Suddenly, he grabbed Johnathan hard by the arm, "Watch this, boy."

He threw the meat over the side of the ship into the ocean. The water that had been dark blue, turned almost white; all the boy could see were large fish fighting over the meat; then it was over as quickly as it had begun.

Now the captain turned to Johnathan with less than a friendly face. "Those would be sharks; they are really fond of little boys. Do you know what I mean?"

Johnathan was too frightened to answer. He stared at the sea where the sharks had been. "That could have been me, he thought." The captain had saved his life once again. The captain let go of Johnathan who went over to the main mast and sat down. Still shaking over the thought of what could have happened, there he sat for the rest of the day. Over to the port side, Johnathan had watched the sleeping dog. At night its head would rise and watch something move on the deck. It would move like the wind and come back with a mouse or something larger. When one of the crew came a little too close, the dog would start to growl. The crew always moved out of the way. They had a lot of respect for the big animal. Johnathan looked at the plate of food that he was given. There was some cheese covered with mold on it. He broke it open. There was a small worm hanging out from the cheese. Johnathan picked the worm out of the cheese. Then he broke a piece off from the moldy mess. He looked around to see if anyone was watching.

He did not think anyone was. But Wink and Mr. Jon were watching. Johnathan threw a small piece next to the dog. Wink started to move toward Johnathan.

Mr. Tom stopped him. "Watch, we will see what happens." The two anticipated a blood bath. The dog opened one of its eyes and watched the cheese. Then he would close his eye. Each time someone walked close to the cheese, again the beast growled. By night the cheese was still there. But when Johnathan woke, the cheese was gone. The dog was in the same place that he had been the night before. Wink was walking over to the boy. He had another plate of cheese and fruit. Wink watched as he walked away from the boy. Mr. Jon waited for Wink. They both watched from the shadows as Johnathan ate the fruit and picked through the cheese.

Johnathan in a quiet voice said "Here, boy," then threw another piece of cheese. It landed next to the dog's head. It slowly reached over and ate the cheese. Johnathan threw another piece a few feet from the dog. "Here, boy," he said. The dog rose up. He walked up to the cheese and ate it. This time Johnathan put a piece in his open hand. "Here, boy," he said. Mr. Jon told Wink, "Let him go. If the sea dog takes Squid's hand, it was not our fault."

Wink grinned, "I am going to like this."

The dog started to walk over toward Johnathan, whose hand was shaking as he waited for the attack. The wire-like hair was standing up on the back of the dog as he came closer. "Here, boy," squeaked Johnathan. The dog was almost on him. Johnathan dropped the cheese from fear. The dog stopped. Johnathan started to pick up the cheese. Before he could, he heard the growl from the beast. Johnathan looked up at the dog who was now looking right down at him. "Here, boy," he picked it up again.

Wink started to giggle. He bit his lip to keep from all out laughter. The dog was only inches from the boy's hand.

"Here, boy, good boy," Johnathan was too scared to move.

Then the dog lunged for the hand. Johnathan was too scared to look. "Do I still have a hand?" he thought. Not a scratch. It happened so fast, Johnathan did not see the dog bite.

The first mate and Wink were extremely disappointed. Mr. Jon put his hand on Wink, "Wait a little longer." The dog started to turn and walk away.

Johnathan quickly broke another piece of cheese off.

"Here, boy," he said. By this time most of the crew were watching and hoping for some excitement. The dog stopped, then turned to see the boy. "Come on, boy, you can have it." This time Johnathan was not frightened. Slowly the dog came up to Johnathan. As it came closer, Johnathan pulled his hand in a little. He held his hand next to his shirt. He was sure the dog could smell his fear. The dog came within inches of the boy. This time his hair was not standing up. It slowly took the cheese from Johnathan, which was quickly replaced with another, then another. Johnathan put his other hand on the dog's head. "Good boy," Johnathan continued to pet the dog as he shared the rest of his food. The boy had finally found a friend, and the beast did also. By this time Wink was angry. He started to yell at the boy. He started to pull his blade as he came for the boy. Johnathan shrugged; he put his hands over his closed eye to protect himself.

The scream was so loud that everyone on the ship heard it. The captain was on deck and able to see the dog had Wink's hand in its mouth, trying to make the nasty pirate drop the blade.

The captain yelled, "Drop your blade man, you bloody fool." Wink released the blade from his bloody hand. As soon as he did, the dog released the man, then backed up to Johnathan. He lay next to the boy. He stayed next to Johnathan until the boy went to sleep with a smile on his face for the first time since he had been kidnapped.

Five days out Johnathan could see land. It was an island on the port side. He thought it was close enough to swim for. But he remembered the last time he tried that. And now he had a four-legged friend.

The pirate captain approached the boy. “In a few days, we will be home. Then we will send word to your uncle to come for you,” said the captain with an evil grin on his face.

“My uncle is already coming,” Johnathan answered.

“Now where do you think he would look for you? We are going to a place next to the Devil himself. Even if your uncle knew where it was, he would not come,” the captain smiled.

The captain started to walk away. Johnathan remembered the story Uncle Jamie had told him about the Island of the Shee and the island south that might be the home of the pirates.

“The Island of the Shee,” Johnathan whispered in a low voice.

The captain stopped only for a second, paused, and then kept walking. He raised his brow as he pondered the remark of his young guest. As he walked by the man sitting by the mast, eating again, he kicked his stool out from under him in a fit of anger.

CHAPTER 9

Only six days out to sea. Jamie knew The Fighting Dove was making good time. The wind propelled the ship through the blue waves. Clouds clothed in white danced over the azure sky. The ocean was as mesmerizing as he could remember. The dolphins frolicked in the water in front of the ship. But no one saw any of the wonders of the sea. They were on a mission. All hands were making ready for war. Jamie was at the helm. Not a word was said that didn't need be. Each one of the crew knew what was at risk; Johnathan. And they would do anything they could to free him. The united crew sailed on.

After sailing all day in the hot sun, the cool darkness was a welcome sight. The ship cut through the sea like a hot knife through butter.

Jamie was standing on the upper deck when Christian came from behind him. "Have you seen the moon, Captain?" he asked. The moon had a pale ring around it as bright as the moon itself.

"I have," Jamie nodded. "I think we may be in for some rough weather. Have the crew make us storm-ready if you would, Christian."

"Aye, Captain," answered Christian.

Another crewman came up to Jamie. "Have you seen the moon, captain?"

Jamie nodded. "Don't make too much of it yet; stay focused man, we have enough to worry about." By morning the wind was gone. The blue sky was replaced with oranges and reds. There were clouds, but they were not moving.

The eastern horizon was covered with clouds. Christian and Jamie were watching the sunrise. "Captain, I think we are in for a storm."

"Aye, this will be a big one. I can smell this one coming. All we can do is wait for it. We will see this one sooner than later." Jamie yelled, "All hands on deck. Make ready for the storm."

"Everything is secure captain," answered Christian.

"Are the sails ready to come down? And are they tight? We don't want to lose a mast." Christian knew they were ready, but he had the men check for one last time. For now, the sea was about to get angry.

By noon the ocean was deceptively flat, like a sorceress forecasting danger. The blue water turned an eerie green that almost glowed. No wind, all that could be done now was watch, wait, and hope. Jamie's mind was all about Johnathan. "I hope that he did not get caught in this storm. If he was, God help him." Soon the wind was starting to pick up. Jamie watched the sails. The ship was now cutting through the ocean of dismal green covered with whitecaps. Still the mysterious glow of a sea that is about to get angry haunted the crew. The sun was now hidden behind the thick black clouds. To the east the sky was dark. Lightning tinkered on the horizon as the crew watched. The air was filled with the friction of the approaching storm. As far as Jamie could see to the northeast and as far to the southeast, the storm was approaching at a much faster rate than he wanted.

The air was thick with the nitrogen smell of the sea. "This is going to be the storm of storms," Jamie said in a calm voice. The white caps on the green sea gave way to darkness as the storm engulfed the ship. The once mighty ship looked small and fragile as it sailed north. Just a day before, the sun had been directly overhead at this time. Now to the west the light was disappearing rapidly. The white caps were now replaced by waves, angry waves that with each minute became more formidable and taller and more menacing. The eastern waves crashed into the ship. Jamie was forced to go northwest and ride the waves. Now the storm was navigating the voyage. The crew had dropped all the main sails and left just enough to stay on course, and they were tight with the wind. They rode the waves while trying to stay on a northern route as much as they could. The light was coming only from the west now, what little could penetrate the storm. As Jamie tried to steer the ship, Christian pointed to the South.

"Captain, waterspout."

"Don't worry about that one Christian. Worry about those two." Jamie pointed to the east, as two funnels slowly dropped down from the clouds. The twin funnel clouds moved toward the ship. Closer and closer they came, about a mile between them. The one to the south was not a threat. But the one to the left of it was headed right for the ship. As the waterspouts closed on the ship, two more dropped down from the clouds, one north and one to the west. Now the ship was right in the center of five waterspouts. The wind screamed at the ship and crew. Each man knew his job and was fighting for his life and the life of the ship.

Jamie yelled, "Make the hatches tight and the lines tighter. Anyone who does not have to be here, go below." The waterspout was closing on the ship, just enough light yet to see the whirlpool at the base of the spout. Then the rain came, the rain of fish. The deck was covered with live fish plucked from the sea. They were jumping for their lives, trying to get off the deck and back to their watery home.

"Mr. Christian, I don't think I have had the pleasure of a rain of fish before."

"Nor I, Captain," answered Christian.

The crew could not focus on the arriving fish! All they could see was the whirlpool under the waterspout closing in on the ship. Some of the men had to put their hands over their ears. The noise of a thousand thunderstorms was almost upon them.

Closer and closer it came. Then with a bounce, the cyclone went right over the mast of the ship. The crew could look up right into the funnel. Then down it came, on the other side of the ship. It was silently watched by all until it was out of sight.

"Captain," yelled Christian. "I will want to get out of this storm, if for no other reason than to tell this story to my grandchildren."

"May you live that long," answered Jamie.

"And you, Captain. And may I say, it would be fine if I never saw another rain of fish."

The waves washed the fish back to the sea. The crew took their turns on deck. Then the next would relieve them. This went on for hours. Except for the captain; he was at the helm, running on excitement and the thought of Johnathan in the same storm. In a cold but stern voice, Jamie spoke. "I hope the pirates outrun the sea this time, for Johnathan's sake. But make no mistake, Christian, I will catch them. The storm is too good for them, compared to what I will do to them." By now the ocean was in control of the ship. The waves pounded the ship. The wind turned the ship around as it was picked up by the waves. Now the waves were coming in broadside. As soon as they turned the ship with the sea, they were picked up again and again.

Jamie yelled to Christian, "I need you here at the helm." The long hours were starting to take their toll on him. Christian was already there. Between the two they brought the helm back under control and took back the ship from the sea.

They put the ship with the storm. "Steer her with the wind and waves, Christian."

"Aye, aye, Captain," answered Christian. The sea played with the ship as if it were a toy. By now the waves were taller than the ship.

Darkness was all around the ship. Night had arrived on time. The storm was as murderous as ever. The clouds opened just for a moment. Moonlight poured down on the sea. The horrified crew watched as the mother of all waves was looking down at them.

"Hold on," yelled Jamie. The ship rose, as the rogue wave lifted the ship higher than the sky. The rudder came out of the sea. Christian and Jamie looked at each other. "Don't let go now, Christian, we are about to go down fast." As soon as Jamie's words left his mouth, the ship fell. He could count his heartbeats as he waited for the ship to smash into the sea. In slow motion, the ship fell slamming into the wave in front of them. Now the ship was broadside to the incoming waves. The ship was starting to roll. "Turn her hard, man," screamed Jamie. The port side of the Dove was almost touching the sea. Slowly the ship righted and was with the wind once again. Down below every man that was not needed sat ready to jump into action in a heartbeat, ready to relieve the next man. No greenhorns here, but some of them looked a little green. Most of the crew had seen the angry sea before. But everyone knew this was as bad as it gets. If fear was among them, they didn't show it; their trust in each other and their captain was extremely evident.

The ship creaked and cracked, but was still watertight. The only water in the ship came in when a hatch was opened. The buckets lay empty next to the crew. So far, they were not needed. But they were ready. Jamie and Christian brought the ship around. They rode the waves again and again when the moon would allow them to see the waves towering above them. They wished that it were dark again. To say visibility was poor was an understatement.

"Mr. Christian, have the crew call out."

"Aye Captain," replied the first mate. One by one the shouts came in.

"Portside, all here, starboard, all here, forward, all here."

"All here, sir," replied Christian. Jamie nodded relieved just a little, upon hearing the news. The noise of the wind and rain was so loud that thinking was out of the question. All of the tumult was soon drowned out. It was coming again. The sound of a waterfall was approaching the ship. Everyone on deck held on.

Jamie yelled, "It seems that the mother of all waves has a sister, hold on!"

CHAPTER 10

Johnathan woke up. There was no dog in sight. He started to look for him. The crew would not come near him, and that was alright with the boy. He picked himself up and looked around. As Johnathan walked down from the main deck looking for his new friend, the thought flashed in his head. "During the night, maybe one of the crew got rid of the dog. But he had not heard anything. The only way they could get rid of the dog was to shoot him. He is much too fast and smart to fall from a knife.

Then one of the crew approached him. Johnathan watched and waited.

"The captain said to give you this. And don't let me find you wasting it. And don't give it to your dog."

Upon hearing this, Johnathan looked up and smiled. He knew that his new friend was still there. He sat down and waited. He sat on the step, next to the rail, then started to eat. As he ate, he could see a shadow on the forward deck. It pounced on a rat. Snapping the neck almost in an instant. Johnathan watched as the beast ripped the rat and ate it. As he ate, he watched the beast rise slowly. He shook his head. When he did so, the drippings from his mouth flew in the air, landing in every direction. Just as it may, Wink was walking close by. He also received some of bloody saliva from the dog. Wink wiped the dog spit from his face and started to raise his hand to the dog to strike it. "You, stupid dog." As soon as the smelly pirate raised his hand, the dog raised up. The dog let Wink know that the stinky human was not in charge. A deep growl issued from the animal, showing all his teeth, his front feet wide apart, his hair on the back of his neck straight up. He was ready to pounce. Johnathan thought that Wink was the stupid one. The pirate slowly lowered his hand and backed away as sweat was running down his face. The rest of the crew laughed. Johnathan also laughed. But not too loud. He had no friends here.

The large dog turned toward Johnathan and started to walk toward him. Johnathan turned white with fear. Now the dog was right in front of him. There was no place to run. The dog came closer, its head down with his eyes watching Johnathan.

Wink started to walk toward the boy. The dog stopped and turned his head with a growl aimed at the sailor. Wink put his hands out in front of him. Palms out, "All right, you can have the little squid." The coward backed away, still sweating as he stumbled over a misplaced rope.

As for the rest of the crew, they kept their distance from the dog. The dog turned for Johnathan one more time, slowly walking closer and closer. Johnathan thought that this was the largest dog that he had ever seen. He was as tall as him when he walked. His hair felt like wire. His coat was a light brown or grey, depending on how the sun was shining on him. But not a solid color. There was no fat on the dog.

One of the crew halfway up the mast yelled, "Looks like the dog is going to get a little squid for lunch." He must have known how scared the boy was. Johnathan could not move. He just sat, waiting for the dog.

The captain had heard the commotion and came for a look-see. He pulled out his pistol and lowered it at the dog.

"The squid, as you say, is more valuable to me than the sea dog." explained the captain. The dog stopped when the captain spoke, he turned and showed his teeth. The men that stood with the captain had backed away.

The dog continued to growl as it came closer to the boy. Now the dog was right in front of Johnathan. It was still growling, but his eyes were on the crew, not Johnathan.

"Don't move, lad," called the captain in a calm voice. He pulled back the hammer on his weapon and made ready to shoot the dog. The dog was inches from the boy's face. Just as the captain was going to pull the trigger, the dog dropped. But there was no gunshot. The dog turned its neck around so as to see the captain and the crew.

The captain lowered his pistol. "I did not see that one coming. It looks like the squid has a dog." The dog continued to growl while looking at the crew, who could not believe what had happened.

Wink was the first of the crew to remark. "Aye, you stupid dog, you can have the squid." Then the crew went about their duties, carefully avoiding the huge animal. After the men scattered, the dog turned and lifted his head to Johnathan. Johnathan, still in a daze did not know what to think. So, he lifted a piece of food and held it out to the dog. It was quickly taken by the dog. Then for the first time since Johnathan was on the ship, something happened. The dog wagged its tail. The captain was still watching. He turned, shaking his head a little, and disappeared in the ship.

The dog lay at Johnathan's feet until the last man had left. Then it stood up and lowered its head and pushed Johnathan in the side. It did this time and time again until Johnathan gave some more of his meal to the dog. Now the dog lay beside Johnathan, drooling ever so much as Johnathan ate. He wiped the drool from his arm and shared the rest of his meal with his new friend. Johnathan would throw food next to his feet. Slowly the dog went down and picked it up. Johnathan's feet were covered in dog spit. He had a little more food left. With the dog's still tail wagging, Johnathan threw it to him. All hands and the captain were now laughing. Thinking that it was over, one of the crew started down the steps on the port side. The dog raised its head and growled. The man went back up and down the other side, giving Johnathan a mean look. Johnathan and his new friend finished their lunch. Then the dog lay down next to the boy. From then on everything that Johnathan did, his new friend did with him. Johnathan always slept on the deck, but now his new friend slept with him.

The next morning the captain came up to Johnathan, "So you and the sea dog seem to hit it off. Maybe you should take care of him."

The boy smiled, "Yes, sir."

"Don't spoil him with food. If you do, he won't catch the mice and rats. He is a fine hunter. The man that let us have him said he had some wolf or something in him. He was cut off a little short and never did say what he meant." Johnathan could tell by the way the captain spoke, that he had killed the dog's owner; it was no wonder the dog did not like anyone on the ship. "Well, the first thing you do is clean up that little mess over there." The captain pointed at the biggest pile of poop Johnathan had ever seen. Johnathan didn't mind cleaning up after his friend. Each time he threw it over the side the yellow-tail snappers must have thought he was throwing candy at them. Each time one of the crew would come close to him, the sea dog would growl-except for the captain, and he would growl at the dog. Johnathan's new friend needed a name. His hair was long, his ears didn't want to stand, he looked like a monster from a scary book that his mother would not let him read.

"I think I will call you Hairy, Hairy the sea dog," said Johnathan to himself.

"Captain, we are leaving the wind," one of the crew yelled.

The captain looked up at the sails. The motionless sails hung there, quiet and still. The captain looked to the south. "There is a large storm brewing there to the south. As soon as it passes, the wind will come back," said the captain.

All day the ship drifted in the hot sun, and the dog lay at Johnathan's feet. "My hairy friend, you must be hot," Johnathan gave him some water.

That night it was still hot. No wind, and the ship drifted. The boy could see lightning from the storm. All night the southern sky delivered flashing fireworks as far as he could see. Hairy and Johnathan watched the storm as the captain walked over.

"I hope for your sake that your Uncle Jamie is not in that storm. No one could survive a storm like that. For a fighting man to be lost at sea, it is not right."

"My uncle will be here! He would not let anything stop him," replied Johnathan. The captain nodded and walked away. The ship drifted through the hot steamy tropical night.

Hairy and the boy fell asleep looking toward the south, watching the storm light up the sky from one end to the other. Johnathan woke up just long enough to say, “Where are you Uncle Jamie?” then went back to sleep.

CHAPTER 11

One thing about the sea; it does not hold a grudge nor stay angered forever. The sun was a pleasant sight. Everyone was on deck exhausted, tired, and hungry. "Set the sails into the wind; we have a boy to find," Jamie commanded. Like clockwork, the sails filled with wind, the ship now moving, cutting the waves with a purpose.

"Take the helm," Jamie told the first mate. Then he went down to the chart room to try to figure out how far they were off course. They had survived the storm of storms, but this mission had not even started yet. Somewhere out there was an island of pirates and a young boy who did not deserve what had happened to him. After calculating three courses, Jamie was sure they were farther away now than when they had started. But considering the storm they had just survived, they were a lucky bunch indeed.

Jamie walked back to the helm and gave the new course. "We will have to make up time," Jamie told the first mate.

"Captain, the sea is a queer thing. All night it didn't want us to make it. But now we have paid our dues; we will find this island. It is the will of the sea.

Jamie looked at the mate and said, "I just hope we are not too late!

Johnathan awoke next to his new friend. The first thing he did was look at the sails just hanging from the mast. He could see all the patches and repairs. As the sun came through the sails, he also could see round holes behind the patches from cannon balls. One of the masts looked like it was a little taller at one time. And the crow's nest had a hole in it. The ship had some history to it. In each part, there was a story. But Johnathan did not want to know of them. The deep blue water was gone now; Johnathan could see the bottom, the water so clear he could see hundreds of feet down. There were patches of seaweed floating on the top of the water. Johnathan could see thousands of small fish gleaming in the sunlight. The ocean was like a mirror. Johnathan walked to the highest point of the deck. He could go anywhere now with Hairy by his side. Hairy did not like anyone else on the ship. And he was not going to let anyone close to Johnathan.

Johnathan looked at Hairy, "I think you are bigger than I am." When the boy looked at the dog, the dog would look right into Johnathan's eyes as if he were trying to understand him. Sometimes the dog would move his head a little clockwise and make a sound like he was trying to say something. Just then the captain walked up to Johnathan. Hairy did not like the captain, but he was the only one on the ship that Hairy would not growl at. He walked in between the boy and the captain. Maybe Hairy knew who was in charge.

"Well, Squid, I don't think your dog would let anything happen to you. Do you have a name for the dog?" asked the captain.

"His name is Hairy," replied Johnathan.

"What is your name captain?' The captain laughed, "Hairy, the sea dog."

Then the captain replied, "I'm Captain LeDuval, some call me the Devil Captain." Just as the captain started trying to walk around the dog to Johnathan, Hairy moved between the boy and the captain. The captain started to walk around the dog, Again the dog stood between the two.

"It seems that you have in fact found a friend." After saying that, the captain walked away.

"Captain we are drifting east too far," the sailor remarked to the captain.

"Don't you think I know that," he growled back. "When the wind comes back, we will set sail for home."

The ship had drifted for days. These were the warmest days and nights that Johnathan could remember. Sometimes he could see blue water, and other times he could see the ocean bottom. Then one morning Johnathan could smell flowers-just like at home. The sun was coming up in the east.

"Land, ho," called the lookout. Every man ran to the port side. There was the southern side of an island.

"Captain, we are on the wrong side of the island," the first mate yelled. "Don't you think I know that," the captain said. The captain was growing tired of being asked questions that each one knew the answer to. "Well, what would you have me do, magically move the ship to the west? Or maybe you all could blow the sails full with your lungs." This time the captain was disgusted. He had no plan. "Just sit and wait for the wind," he said. They drifted for most of the day-still no wind. The sun was ready to set. Clouds filled the sky and the ocean started to show some moonlight through them. Johnathan could see the captain was getting worried.

The lookout yelled, "Fast water ahead."

The captain yelled, "Lower the small boat over the side. Grab what you can."

The captain came over to Johnathan, "Squid, get into the boat." Again, Hairy got between Johnathan and the captain. He would not let the captain close. "Boy, get into the boat! This is your last chance." said the captain. Hairy would not let Johnathan go with the captain. The captain and his men went over the side. They all could not fit in the boat; some were swimming. They watched as the boat tried to row toward the island.

"Hairy, why did they all leave so quickly?" They were all alone on the ship!

As they heard waves crashing on the rocks the two ran to the front of the ship. Ahead of them was an ocean river running between the two islands.

The ship was starting to steer west toward the rocks. South of the rocks were the pirates, who were headed toward the sandy beach. North of the beach was over a mile of rocks and boulders being hammered by the sea.

Soon the ship was caught in the stream. The ship was being pushed not to the shore but going right for the North side of the rocks. Then the screams started. All Johnathan could do was hold on to Hairy and wait for the crash.

The captain's boat was almost out of sight. They were trying to get to the beach but headed for the rocks on the shoreline. As the waves crashed on the rocks. Johnathan could also hear the small boat crashing. He could hear the men yelling to each other. He could not be sure if they made it because it was starting to get dark. The screams increased with both intensity and in numbers. Now it was dark, and the ocean became rough! The ship was going sideways to the port, closer and closer to the next island to the north. The ocean sounded like a river. Hairy started to growl. Then Johnathan could hear the screams from the island north of the one that the pirates had landed on. The pirate ship hit a large rock. The main sail came down. Each rock pushed the ship closer to the next island to the north. They were at the edge of the ocean river. Just then the ship hit another rock, throwing it into calm water north of the stream. The ship had started to move a little when the two could feel it stop. Johnathan held on to Hairy, who stood right next to him. The ship shook and screeched, then exploded on the rocks under the pressure of the seawater. The deck under the two shattered, leaving about a six by eight-foot piece of deck with a rail on one side. Johnathan held the rail with one arm and with the other he held Hairy with all his strength. They watched as the ship fell apart. The terrified boy was too scared to cry. The only sound he could hear above the crashing waves was the screams from the island.

"Hairy, I don't think I like this, not at all," whimpered Johnathan. Just then what was left of the ship broke in half. The ship was starting to slip into the sea. The screams were closer and so loud that the two turned away so that their ears wouldn't hurt so bad. All that was left of the pirate ship was part of the deck and some railing. Johnathan held Harry tight as they flowed in the river between the islands.

Hairy was starting to growl. He saw something, but it was too dark to tell what it was. Something grey came out of the water next to the raft. It was alive It was like some kind of sea monster. The long arm had two holes in the end of it. Just then, it shot water and air out of the long grey arm.

Then a scream right next to the raft deafened them. Johnathan looked over next to the monster. In the moonlight, he could see two eyes staring at him in the darkness. Hairy was barking, his teeth were showing in the moonlight. Over where the two eyes are, the monster was looking at them. On the other side were two more eyes and another grey arm.

The screams stopped.

All they could hear was the shoreline ahead and the waves hitting the sand. The raft went right past the rocks, in and out, back and forth, right up to the shore.

Then there was the jungle. Johnathan wanted to run. Hairy and Johnathan jumped off the raft. It slowly went back out to sea never to be seen again. In the moonlight, they could see eyes on both sides of them. If they moved the eyes went with them. So, they sat there, Hairy stopped barking. But he would not let the grey monsters get close to the boy.

CHAPTER 12

Captain LeDuval and most of his men made it to shore. Their cove was on the other side of Pirate Island. They had no choice but to build a fire for the night and listen to the sound of the Shee. Not only had they lost their ship, they had lost their hostage. "As soon as the light comes up, we will have to make our way through the jungle. We should be on the other side by nightfall," the captain said in a calm voice.

They rested but did not sleep. The screaming stopped when the moon was high above them; now the tranquil night was as eerie as the screams. They stared into the darkness until first light. The fog was lifting, for one of the pirates yelled, "Captain, our ship, it is still afloat!" As they looked at the ship it turned and twisted in the sea. It was only half there. The rest of the ship was gone.

"She was a good one, she was," Captain LeDuval looked at his men, scratching his head, "I think we can get to her one last time." The water between the islands was as calm as the captain had ever seen. You could almost walk across the rocks to get to the ship's remains. "She won't last forever; I think that now is the time, Maybe the little squid is still on board." One of the pirates worked his way out to the ship. The tide was low and the current was soft. "Hurry now," the captain knew that this reprieve would not last. They tied a rope from the ship to the shore and quickly took everything that was of value to them, weapons, food, and gear. Most of the supplies were lost in the storm.

"No Squid, Captain," said one of the pirates. "He must have fallen off in the night."

One of the men said, "Captain hear that?" Everyone went quiet. "It is the Squid's Sea Dog. Maybe he made it." Looking at the shoreline of the Island of the Shee, it was clear sand all around the shore, but compared to the shoreline of the Pirates Island that showed there is nothing but jungle for the unlucky visitor. The water was even lower now than before. What was normally a river was now a creek.

The captain looked at the men, "I think that we should go and save the Squid. It is our duty, don't you think." He asked with a smile."

"Captain, that is the Island of the Shee; only the Devil himself would go there," said the fat pirate. The captain was looking the other way when the man spoke, and drawing his pistol from his belt, turned and placed a lead ball through the fat man's head.

"Now, he might be right, but consider this; I am right here, the choice is yours." The men started to pack; next stop; the Island of the Shee.

CHAPTER 13

Jamie knew he had to make up for lost time. His ship had been blown hundreds of miles off course. But they were alive. He had not heard of anyone surviving such a storm. He needed to make haste. He headed the ship north, trying to get into the trade winds. "This was no place for a boy, a boy with a bunch of cut-throats," he thought. There was some damage to the sails and the mast. The crew repaired them as they sailed. The ship was taking on a little water but not enough to slow them down. There would be time to chink the sides when they got back.

Jamie told the first mate, "Now we have the wind, let's see what she can do. She is a good ship and she won't let us down." The sails flapped just a little then filled out. The ship started to cut the waves like butter. At this rate, they would make course in record time.

"Captain what are we in for?" asked one of the crew.

Jamie looked at the man. "That is an honest question, and you will get an honest answer. The island is about twenty-five miles north and south, and about twenty miles east to west. It sits between two larger islands. On the east side, you have high waves and rocks. On the west side, you have coral reefs. On the east side, you would crash on the rocks. On the west side you hit the reefs," continued the captain.

"But Captain, how do we get ashore?" asked the sailor.

"We don't, at least not there," said the captain. "Now this Island of the Shee sits between the two larger islands. There is just enough space between for the ocean in the east to flow to the ocean on the west. The current is fast and don't forget the rocks. That is one ocean stream we will not try to cross. The island that we are going to is the island to the south of the Shee. As long as we don't go too far to the north and get caught in the stream, we will find the home of the pirates. Should not be too hard; we just sail up the west side of the island until we see where the pirates' camp is," said Jamie.

"Then what," asked the sailor?

"Then we fight," Jamie smiled sternly and reached out and put his hand on the man's shoulder. They just looked at each other for a moment and then looked out to sea.

CHAPTER 14

All night Johnathan watched the two sets of eyes as they seemed to float over the beach. Not getting any closer or any further away, they just watched. It was a very long, warm night indeed; Johnathan held on to his four-legged friend. Finally, the sun was coming up over the ocean. The sky was on fire. The rocks out to sea were dark shadows in the morning light. It looked like the rocks were to be on fire with the sunrise. The sky was also on fire while small puffy clouds covered the horizon. The morning breeze was full of the fragrances of the Caribbean-jasmine, mango, bougainvillea. Johnathan watched the sky start to turn an indigo blue. Hundreds of rocks, small ones, just touched the surface of the waves, while other big ones appeared like small islands. The waves hit the rocks and splashed well over the top, turning into white foam. The symphony that Johnathan listened to all night was now visible. Now the sky was getting lighter, from dark blue to light azure. For the first time, Johnathan could see the sand. It looked like a rose color or coral.

Just then Johnathan remembered, "Where are the watchers?" Hairy was starting to growl. They could see footprints in the sand coming closer and closer.

"Danny, keep Tinker back, you are starting to scare the boy," came a voice from nowhere.

Johnathan's heart was pounding as he grabbed Hairy. "Who is it," as Johnathan hugged the dog, he had tears running down his face. Hairy was ready for a fight; when he showed his teeth, the footprints stopped.

Then another voice from the other side of Johnathan said, "Naughty, I was just getting a closer look, I don't think this one is a pirate." These two voices were now fighting with each other from both sides of Johnathan.

"I'm not a pirate!" Johnathan yelled.

Then right before Johnathan, tracks in the sand started to run right for them; this time Hairy's tail was wagging. Johnathan must have looked dumbfounded. The tracks were right in front of the boy, dancing around in a circle. Johnathan started to giggle, just a little, and he could feel the wind from something close by, but still could not see what or who was standing there. Johnathan reached out slowly, but nothing. He reached out from side to side, but nothing. Then he looked down between his feet, the prints in the sand went right up to his feet. Slowly he watched as the sand moved just a little. "Maybe there is a snake under the sand," he thought. He very slowly put his shaking hand down to the beach, now the sand had stopped moving. Johnathan stopped and looked at Hairy; he was standing right next to him with his tail going back and forth in the wind. "This is not a game, Hairy," he said. Then on both sides of the boy, he could hear giggles.

Johnathan reached down, not seeing anything but sand. Something was there between him and the sand. "I cannot touch the sand, there is something in the way," thought Johnathan. Then a blast of air blew sand all over Johnathan and Hairy. Johnathan fell backward. Now all around Johnathan, he could hear laughter. Then the sand was moving around where the laughing was coming from. Johnathan reached down and filled his hands with sand, then threw it in the direction of the voices. It looked like some kind of animal, not much bigger than Hairy. But it had a long nose, a really long nose. Just like the ones next to the raft last night. Then the animal shook off all the sand and again disappeared. Johnathan could not see him any longer.

"Danny, tell him or I will be the one to tell him,"-a voice said.

"What is your name, boy; we already know your dog is Hairy." Johnathan did not say anything. He just stood with his mouth open.

"Would you like to see my Doggy?" came the voice. Slowly Johnathan raised his head up and down as he stood up.

"Very well boy, meet Doggy." Just a few feet in front of Johnathan a small creature that looked like an elephant stood in front of him. First, there were tracks and now there was this animal about the size of Hairy. Or maybe just a little bit bigger. Johnathan fell back again. Then the laughing started again.

"Doggy is my elephant," said the voice, Danny's elephant is Tinker," said the voice. Just then there were two animals standing on both sides of Johnathan. Doggy had a spot right over his eye, just like a dog would. Johnathan looked at Tinker; she had no spots, she just looked happy to see them. Then Tinker put her head down, her feet forward, and threw her back feet in the air while she was making circle after circle. Both elephants were now playing with Hairy. Johnathan had never seen Hairy so happy. Johnathan sat on the beach in wonderment watching them play.

To his left, a voice said, "I think Hairy found a new friend." Johnathan looked up at the ocean, by this time the most perfect blue and green, with seaweed floating on top of the water. Johnathan slowly turned his head to the left. Right next to him was a girl. She was no more than three feet tall.

"Are you hungry?" and she handed Johnathan some fruit. He took it, he was starving. When Harry smelled the mango, he rolled on his back until Johnathan shared. The bright reddish, fresh fruit was almost more than he could stand.

She giggled.

Then on the right side of Johnathan, a voice said, "My name is Danny." Johnathan turned to the right, there sitting next to him was a boy not much bigger than the girl.

"We call her Naughty; welcome to our island," said Danny.

Johnathan just sat there looking at both little people while they ate the mango, as the yellow juices dripped down his chin. They could not be more than three feet tall or so. And right in the middle of their forehead was a vertical small raised part. Their skin was almost like a greenish tan.

"What is your name?" asked Naughty.

Hairy liked the mango also. He sat looking at Johnathan till he gave him some more. Johnathan gave Hairy the fruit without speaking or taking his eyes off the girl.

Then Naughty said, "What isss yourrr nameee boyyyy?"

"Jonathan." He said quickly, still in shock.

Danny looked at her and said, "Will you quit teasing Johnathan; he looks like he has had a bad time. Well, Johnathan, what are we going to do with you?" said Danny.

Naughty's face lit up, "Can we keep him?" Johnathan looked back and forth as they talked.

"Johnathan, how did you get here?" Danny asked.

"Pirates. They kidnapped me, but Uncle Jamie is coming for me."
"Johnathan, where are the pirates now?"

"They left me on the ship and went for shore before the ship hit the rocks," said Johnathan.

"Why would they leave you?" asked Naughty.

"Hairy would not let them touch me. They made it to shore on the other island," he pointed to the South. For the first time, Danny and Naughty were not smiling.

Danny jumped to his feet, and whistled, Tinker and Doggy came running. "Naughty, help me cover all the tracks except for Hairy and Johnathan's."

They quickly covered their tracks. "Let's go, Johnathan; we have some pirates to take care of," said Naughty. Johnathan followed Naughty into the jungle. Into the jungle, they went. Then Doggy and Tinker followed jumping and playing, with Danny covering all their tracks except for the newcomers'.

CHAPTER 15

The Devil Captain stood on the beach watching the last man come through the stream of water between the two islands. The water had already started to rise. The ocean river between the two islands had once again become angry. No one could come through the waves now. “Leave the supplies here; just take what we need to find Squid; pistols, food, and rope,” he said. The captain started to walk to the east of the island, along the beach. He looked at the ocean, with the waves hitting the rocks as far as he could see. “I don’t think the Squid could survive that ocean in the day or the night.” They kept walking.

They walked for almost a mile. “Captain! tracks in the sand, the sea dog, and Squid. They go into the jungle,” exclaimed Smoll.

The captain stared at the jungle. He scratched his beard. “Now why would Squid go into the jungle, I think he would be smarter than that? It will be dark soon; we will spend the night on the beach. Set up a lookout port and starboard. And build a fire. Maybe Squid will see the fire and come back to us,” the captain smiled. His crew shook their heads in agreement with the captain. Everyone was happy not to go into the jungle that night.

CHAPTER 16

The wind was pushing Jamie's ship north right up the tropics. They had never made better time than this; deep blue water and a proper wind. The ship cut through the waves and glided over the sea. Small white clouds wandered from one side of the sky to the other. The dolphins were playing with the ship as it cut the waves. Jamie proudly looked at his crew. He was proud of each one of them. They were family.

"Captain, she is a good ship. We paid our dues to the sea, now the sea will give back," said the first mate foretold.

"Never trust the sea," said Jamie. "She can be very good to you, then turn in a heartbeat. I just hope the sea is good to Johnathan."

Then the lookout shouted, "Captain, ship on the port side."

Jamie yelled, "What flag does she fly?"

"No colors, Captain," said the lookout.

"Man, the guns look alive," Jamie noticed. "Is that the ship that paid us a visit?" asked Jamie.

"No, captain, but she doesn't look friendly," warned the lookout.

"Head west by north and cut her off," instructed Jamie.

"Don't give her a target just yet."

"Gunners prepare to take down her mast."

"Aye, aye, captain."

"When I give the order, hard to starboard and give her a full broad side of lead. And I will take care of the wind," yelled Jamie.

As the ships came closer to each other, the sailors saw the crew running over the deck. The strange ship was headed south, as fast as she could. Just then her colors went up; "Pirates!"

Captain Jamie James turned the ship to hard starboard, "Fire!" he commanded. As the ship turned broadside, all the cannons fired just like clockwork. All three masts came down. And there was a small fire on the deck. The pirate ship never got off a good shot. Jamie said, "Let her drift, we have other things more important. I'm sure someone else will take care of her for us."

Jamie headed north; no time wasted; no time gained.

CHAPTER 17

Johnathan quickly twisted his way through the jungle. Tinker and Doggy crushed down the luxuriant plant life as they walked behind in the new path. Hairy was always close behind Johnathan, smelling the jungle floor.

Danny turned and said, "Let's stop here," and so they rested.

Naughty opened her pouch and gave Johnathan some more fruit.

"What kind of food is this," he questioned.

Naughty looked at Johnathan, "There is only one other place you can find it. This fruit and green moss came from our homeland many years ago. It is our favorite food."

"It is very good; I have never eaten anything like it. Where is your homeland? And how did you get here?" prodded Johnathan. Danny looked at Naughty and shook his head as if to say. You have told him too much already."

"Johnathan have you ever heard of a Banshee," asked Naughty?"

"Oh, God, now you have done it," Danny replied as he continued to move his head.

"Now, Danny," Naughty looked at him with her smile. "I don't want Johnathan to get the wrong impression or to mix us up with something else. Johnathan," Naughty looked right at him, "Have you ever heard this before." Then she screamed just like the night before when Johnathan and Hairy were on the raft.

Johnathan put his hands over his ears, Hairy put his head on the ground with his paws over it, "Yes," he moaned."

Danny laughed, "Don't look at me. Only the lasses can do it; are you impressed?"

Johnathan nodded his head, yes.

Danny said, "Well, Naughty, are you going to show him any more secrets?"

When Johnathan turned to her, she was gone. "Where did she go?" Johnathan asked.

"Johnathan, I'm still here. Now watch closely." Naughty was not there; then slowly you could see her shadow. Then she was there.

"How did you do that?" Johnathan asked.

"Don't know really, we have just always been able to do it."

Now Johnathan looked at the two of them, only about three-feet-tall or so, and greenish dark skin with a little vertical raised spot on their forehead above the eyes. Danny was just a little taller than Naughty. But Naughty was very pretty. He felt very good with her unless she screamed again.

"Danny, can you go away too; without leaving?" Johnathan asked.

"Watch this." He put his hand next to a green fern. His hand turned the same color as the fern. "See, I'm still here, I just tricked your eyes."

"Then on the raft, all I saw was your eyes," replied Johnathan. Naughty laughed. "Yes, that is all."

"But how did Tinker disappear and Doggy?" Johnathan asked.

"Whoever or whatever we touch can become the land around them. But one of us has to touch them."

"Could you make me go away?" Johnathan wondered.

Danny reached over to touch the boy. "No, let me," Naughty said. Naughty looked at Johnathan and smiled. "Now, Johnathan, relax, you will feel warm at first; now watch." She reached out and put her hand on his shoulder. Then he started to blend in with the jungle. Johnathan watched as he became the same color as the jungle, except for his clothes. They were the same. She took her hand off the boy and he could slowly see himself again.

"How come your clothes changed, and mine didn't?" queried Johnathan.

"Our clothes are made out of animal skin, and rubbed with the moss and fruit that we eat.," Naughty explained.

Danny just looked at her. "Naughty, I think you pretty much covered it. Are you happy?"

She smiled, "Johnathan would just have figured it out anyway. Now what are we going to do with the pirates?"

"Naughty, tonight you just scream, and maybe Tinker and I will pay a visit to the pirates. Johnathan, would you like to watch; Can you keep your wolfhound quiet?"

"Why did you call Hairy a wolfhound," Johnathan asked.

Naughty looked at Danny, "And you were saying?"

Danny continued; "At our homeland, sometimes, the people would use this kind of dog to hunt us down, to kill us because we are different from them. They never caught one of us, but we got a bit of a bite now and then. They are real hunters. Once they get going, you can hardly stop them from killing their prey. They called them wolfhounds.

Johnathan looked at Hairy who dropped his head down as if he knew what they were talking about. "Hairy is not that kind of dog."

Danny looked at Johnathan, "is he the kind of dog that will be quiet tonight when we scare the pants off those pirates?

"Yes," said Johnathan.

Both Danny and Naughty just looked at the boy and smiled.

"Tonight, we scare; tomorrow, we go home. I think we may need some help tonight. I'll take care of it; I'll be back in a wee bit."

CHAPTER 18

The sunlight was about gone. The pirates had a large fire on the beach. They could hear the waves hitting the rocks, but all they could see was dark water on the horizon. The sky was darker, and the clouds were on fire. Slowly the clouds turned into trails of wind moving across the moonlight. The shadows loomed over the rocks that lined the horizon. There was one man on each side of the beach with a smaller fire to keep warm and look for trouble.

Just then, the night opened up as a terrifying scream so loud that all the animals sleeping in the jungle were awakened; birds that were silent were now flying for their lives.

All the pirates were now on their feet. They were ready for a fight, but unsure of whom they were ready for or why they were ready. All of them were frightened. The screams kept coming. The captain fired a shot into the jungle. All he heard was a laugh and more screams. The pirate at the south fire was looking, straining his eyes. Then out of nowhere something long and grey hit him. His feet went over his head. The captain was unable to see where his man was. He sent two men to check on him.

"How could anyone sleep with that screaming going on?" he thought. They came back, dragging the crewman between them. His face was black and blue from being hit with something large. He was incoherent and babbling about invisible monsters. Suddenly, all on the beach could hear the guard on the north beach hit the ground.

The captain ordered the underlings, "Go and get him." This time, not being totally irrational, four of the men went. When they came back, the story was just the same. They dragged the man back to the fire. They threw water on the man to wake him up. No one else went out from the big fire that night. But the screams kept coming for some time

CHAPTER 19

Jamie was in the captain's quarters; the first mate was with him. "We should see Pirate's Island soon; not too close we don't want to be blown out of the water before we get there."

"Captain," a sailor rushed in. "We have a ship on the horizon."

Jamie and the first mate went to the helm deck. "Lookout, is she friendly?"

"Aye, sir, she is," the lookout answered.

"Never be too safe; all men on deck," ordered the captain.

As the ships grew closer, Jamie could see the ship and her captain. They guided the ships as close as possible to each other.

They were within shouting range. The captain yelled, "Ahoy, Jamie, have you seen a three-sail ship heading south? They had a day's jump on us."

Jamie smiled, "Old friend, the only ship we saw was yesterday. But when we left her, we made sure that she did not have any sails or masts for that matter. Be careful, my friend, and have a safe journey." Jamie went back to his charts.

"And you, old friend." The captain of the ship turned to the helmsman and muttered, "That is one man I would not want to be mad at me." The helmsman shook his head. And they went south to pick up the trail of the pirate ship.

The Fighting Dove, headed north towards the Pirate's Island, was now within sight of the hideaway.

"There she is Captain. The Pirate Island," called the lookout.

Jamie said, "Look for a bay or lagoon with no beach, probably mangrove or rocks. Let's take her slow. Have the guns ready. And let's keep out of harm's way.

"Captain, why no beach?" asked the first mate.

Jamie replied, "If they have a sea wall, the sand will wash out to sea and not come back."

As the ship went up the coastline, one of the crew said, "Look, Captain, a camp."

Jamie looked, "There is something not right about that camp. Let us take the small boat over the side and check it out." The crew dropped the boat over the side, and Jamie and eight men rowed the boat into the cove. The water was clear; the coral and the sand glimmered like jewels and gold scattered on the bottom of the small bay. The water was much too shallow; the small boat almost touched, but they reached the shore unharmed.

"Now be careful; there might be traps." Jamie looked for anything that was not right. The camp looked like a decoy. "They were trying to get some fools to bring their ship in here," he contemplated. Just then one of the men tripped over a vine that was covered in the sand. The vine snapped straight up, just missing the foot of the sailor who tripped it.

"Enough of this; back to the ship," ordered Jamie. And they were off the beach, back to the ship. The tide was going out; they made deep water just in time. "We must be close," said Jamie. "All hands be ready, ready for anything."

Up the coastline they went, until Jamie could see where the end of the island loomed. It looked like a river running ran between this island and the next. "We need to stay away from that island," said Jamie. He was just about to go hard to port when suddenly a hidden bay was hiding from view. "That is where we are going. Not visible from the sea, it is the perfect place for a hidden base. And look, there is deep water," said Jamie.

The first mate said, "Captain, no beach to starboard."

Jamie took the spyglass. "That is their base. Their ship is not here so let's go take a closer look." They lowered the small boat and slowly made the trip up the tropical river flowing from the center off the pirate's island, carefully not setting off any traps. They reached the shore next to a makeshift dock almost invisible to passing ships.

On the shore Jamie and his men found the pirate's site. "Not a pirate to be found, what now?" said one of the crew.

"Back to the ship; all we can do now is wait," responded Jamie.

He took the ship to the mouth of the pirate bay and dropped anchor. The bay was calm, the beach was wide everywhere except the dock. But sailors could not see it from the sea as there were mountains surrounding the bay. "This is the perfect bay; it has to be the pirates, but where are they?" thought Jamie. "If they come back, they would have to get past us first," so they waited.

CHAPTER 20

Johnathan and his new friends slept on the beach, far away from the pirates. As soon as the sun rose, they were off for a tour of the small people's island home. "Come on, Johnathan, would you like to see our island." Naughty waved her hand to follow.

The new friends went into the jungle and up the path to the mountain as they climbed to the top where there was a ridge around the inside of the crater. Johnathan could not see over the ridge because of the clouds in the center.

"Come on, Johnathan," Danny jumped over the side, then Naughty and then Tinker and Doggy. "Johnathan, jump!" a voice merrily called out. Johnathan didn't jump; he just slid down the side, right into a rushing pool of water. Hairy followed. "What kind of place is this?" Johnathan asked.

"A place like nothing you have ever seen," said Naughty. "Come on; we will show you." This had to be the best place that Johnathan had ever been. Anyone could see the sky, but from the ridge above no one could see you from below. They swam over to the water's edge. "Now grab a fern, Johnathan, the biggest one you can find. We are going to show you the island," said Naughty. At the edge of the pool was a runoff. Tinker went first, then Doggy. Danny said, "Now, watch and do the same thing." He put the leaf down and sat on it. Then he was gone. The swift water washed him away.

"Now you do it, Johnathan," said Naughty. Johnathan sat down on the largest broad leaf that he could find, and he was gone, with Naughty right behind. Hairy ran and barked and swam right behind.

Round and round the top of the crater they went. Danny was waiting for them, grinning like a kid on a playground. "Would you like to go a little bit more?" Danny picked up his broad leaf, and walked up the hill a little, where more warm water was rising from the crater. He put his leaf in the water, and off he went again.

Naughty said, “Go on, Johnathan, this is how we get around the island. There are hot springs all around the ridge. You can do this all day. This is how we watch our island. When you think that you are going to stop, there is always another spring to ride.” Clear on the other side of the island, they stopped. “Well, what do you think?” asked Naughty.

Johnathan grinned. Then he exclaimed, “That was the best time I have ever had.”

They walked up to another flat area. “This is where we grow some of our fruits and moss,” said Naughty.

Johnathan looked as far as he could at the endless garden of fruit and moss. Noting from here, he could see every place on the island. He could see the island to the north with the river of sea flowing past on the rocks. “No one could get through that,” he thought.

“What is on that island?” asked Johnathan. He pointed to the island to the north.

Danny said, “There is a tribe of people on that island. They eat just about anything.”

“Oh, that’s nice!” Johnathan wryly answered.

Danny said again, “Anything.”

“Even people?” Johnathan asked, afraid of the answer.

Naughty shook her head and gave Johnathan a disapproving look. “Let’s not go there today. Sometimes when the ocean is calm just before a storm, they come looking for trouble,” said Naughty.

“They find it, too,” said Danny. Danny offered a distraction, “Johnathan, would you like to follow the stream around the mountain again?”

“Yes, but I think that I will need a new leaf. He held it up. Johnathan looked at Danny, grinning through the hole in the middle of the leaf.” After finding a new sturdier leaf, they were off again. All the way around the island, each time they were almost out of water, they would find another underground geyser shooting up from the ground. The water was warm as it came out. Each time it propelled them up enough to carry them on their way. Johnathan laughed so hard his sides were hurting. There were dams every so often made of bamboo. It looked like his friends could raise them with a lever. Why, he didn't know. But it was a ride of a lifetime, with two elephants, one dog, and his two new friends.

This time they had made it all the way back to the starting point. "What a ride," Johnathan laughed, but by now Johnathan was very tired. As they sat next to the pool Johnathan asked, "How did you two get here?"

"On a ship just like you," said Naughty. No one knew we were on it. There was little to eat at home, so we stole away. And here we are."

"How long have you been here?" asked Johnathan.

Danny looked down and said, "A very long time. We missed our friends, but this is better than the place from which we came."

"Did you bring anything with you?" Johnathan asked.

"Some fruit, moss, and a few potatoes; everything else we have here." Danny went over to the edge of the water and went into a cave. In a few moments, he returned with two knives and belts.

"Do you think we need them?" asked Naughty.

"They are pirates," Danny replied. "Need I say more?" So just in case, he handed one set to Naughty.

She strapped the belt on her little frame. "Johnathan, we will stay here tonight."

He followed them into a small cave. Inside the cave was just about everything castaways could want, even a place for a fire. "How old are you two?" Johnathan asked.

Naughty raised her eyes, "How old do you think we are?"

"I would guess that you are a little older than I am. Are you older than ten?" he asked. This time Danny was rolling around on the ground. "Naughty, are you ten?" Danny asked.

"Johnathan we are much older, but we don't age the same as you" Why, my father is over a hundred years old," said Naughty.

"Do you miss him? I miss my family," he said sadly and quietly.

She just smiled, "He is always with me."

"I know what you mean; I could see my Uncle Jamie in my mind telling stories of this island. I can't wait to tell him about you," replied Johnathan.

Naughty looked right at Johnathan, "You can never tell anyone about us. That is why we left home in the first place. People were scared of us. They tried to hunt us down with their dogs. We just want to be left alone, Johnathan. If you tell your uncle, everyone will know we are here. Then they will come and hunt us." Danny sat there shaking his head, yes.

"Promise, you will not tell, it is very important."

Johnathan looked right at the two and said, "I promise."

CHAPTER 21

By this time the pirates were making plans. The captain drew a map in the sand. "The dog has to be with the boy. Half of you go up the beach and the rest come with me. Look for a path into the jungle. When you find a path, fire one shot into the air, and I mean in the air. If a pistol round comes my way, I will take it very personally." He raised his only brow of his eye and stared at the men, "Any questions?"

"No sir," came the answer from all the crew.

"Then let's go," said the captain impatiently. Captain LeDuval took half of the men and went south. The rest went north. About half a mile south the captain found footprints in the sand right next to the jungle. But once in the jungle, there was nothing. "Could this be a trap? I have never seen prints like this." It was a four-legged animal, but the prints were too large for any beast that he had ever seen. The captain scratched his head. He did not look; he just fired a shot. A seagull fell to the ground.

"Good shot, sir," said one of the crew. He turned toward one of the other crewmen, "Now that was some good shooting."

They all agreed. Soon the rest of the crew were there. "We are going into the jungle. Look for anything a broken branch, leaf, or footprint." Then they were off. They left the coral-colored sand and a few palm trees. Then they were in the jungle. Each man's eyes were wide open; they could hear all kinds of strange animal noises. Tropic birds and other species that they were unfamiliar with.

One crewman was called Dirty, and for good reason; he made the rest of the crew look clean. He seemed to draw all the bugs his way from the rest. "Dirty, my man, said the captain. Would you watch aft? Now don't walk too close to the rest of us. That way you can spot trouble."

Dirty said, "Aye, Captain, you count on me, sir."

After he was far behind, the captain said, "It seems that Dirty has taken the bugs with him." They kept going. They found a small freshwater pool and waterfall. The captain bent down to taste the water. "She is good enough for me. Have a drink and make it snappy. The quicker we get back to our island the better." Not much light made it through the jungle. It was hard to stay on course; the captain just kept going up. At least he could see the island better from there. They were about half the way up a path that looked as if something had used it within the past few hours.

"Captain, do you here that noise; it sounds like a waterfall coming right at us." Just when the captain looked up, he could see a wall of water coming right at him. "Run!" the captain yelled. But it was too late; the water picked them off the ground and washed them down the side of the mountain. At the bottom of the mountain, they tumbled right at Dirty's feet. "It would be a real shame if you got wet, wouldn't it," said the captain, as he smashed a bug on his face.

Dirty just smiled, "Haven't seen anything, sir."

The captain growled and smiled while he tilted his head, "Keep up the good work, Dirty. This time let us look for a different way to get up the mountain," mused the captain.

CHAPTER 22

As Johnathan awoke, the sun was already up, and he was alone. Hairy was even gone. He walked out to see where everyone was. He could hear Danny and Naughty laughing. "Well, top of the morning to you, Johnathan. We were just washing some dirt down the mountain," said Naughty. "It will be a while before they try that again. It's just not proper to try to sneak up the mountain like that." Each time the pirates would find another path, Danny and Naughty would open the bamboo dams and wash them back down the mountain. This was great fun; each time was better than the last. Danny wondered why the pirates did not learn the lesson.

"Did you see the man at the far end? The water always stopped before he was wet, as if the water feared him," Danny laughed. "Today, Johnathan, we will show the pirates a good place to swim." They grabbed some large leaves. Danny put his hand out. "Let Doggy go first," he said. Danny whistled and both tiny elephants came running, Doggy first, then Tinker. Doggy went to the edge of the pool, put his head down, kicked up his back feet, turned a circle and was gone. Tinker was right behind.

"They seem happy," Johnathan said. And they followed down the slide of water. Each time when he thought he was at the end of the ride, fresh water from the ground took them back up and the journey continued. The shoreline was visible at every curve of the ride. But first, they had to get some fruit. They slowed down at the garden. Doggy and Tinker were already there. As they approached the pool's edge Doggy put his head down on the sand and shook his tail end just like a dog.

Hairy would hear something in the jungle's edge. And he was gone, chasing the hidden wonders. "Where did Hairy go?" asked Naughty.

"Oh, he is not into fruit that much. He probably found something to eat. The pirates kept him just to rid the ship of rats," Johnathan replied.

"Johnathan, we need to keep a closer watch on him. There is a lot of small life around here that are our friends and need to be protected," said Naughty. "I will try," Johnathan said.

"Let's go, Naughty," said Danny. "We have to show Johnathan our fishing pool." As the pirates kept going around the island, Danny and Naughty were always one step ahead. This time they walked down the mountain just off the side of the beach. You could see a bay of rose-colored sand with palm trees scattered throughout the beach. The rugged mountain range was visible over the beach. Again, the bay water was so clear that they could see the bottom from the mountainside.

"Are we going to the beach?" asked Johnathan.

"Not today," Danny said. "First we have to get rid of the pirates."

Right at the end of the jungle was a freshwater pond, one side of the pond in the jungle, the other in the sand. "What a nice pond!" exclaimed Johnathan.

"Johnathan, do not go too close to the pond; we don't want you to fall in." Hairy went up to the edge of the water. A goldfish was swimming near him. The fish was only about a foot long. Hairy had him. He brought the fish up to Johnathan.

"Well, I have not seen that before," said Danny. Hairy set the fish down next to Johnathan.

"Don't move, Johnathan," said Naughty. She pulled out a knife from her sheath. She stabbed the fish and made sure it was dead. "This is the only place on the island where we have found this kind of fish. We call it a vampire fish. It has two fangs on the upper part of the fish's mouth. One bite and you are gone. See how it can close its mouth and the fangs go right into two holes in the bottom of the mouth; you don't want to pick this one up. Now watch this!" Naughty threw the fish into the pool. The other vampire fish ate it. After the frenzy of the attack, all there was left was blood on the water. "These fish are mean. Now, Johnathan, give me your shirt," said Naughty.

Johnathan gave Naughty what was left of his shirt. She took the shirt and laid it by the edge of the water. It looked like it had been left there on purpose. She even folded it a little. Now let's cover all the tracks except for Johnathan's and Hairy's," said Naughty. They should be here soon. Let's get up the mountain and watch. The four walked up the side of the mountain out of sight of the beach. Danny looked at Doggy and pointed up the mountainside. Both elephants slowly walked up the mountain.

"They did not look very happy," Johnathan said. Johnathan put his arm around Hairy and held him.

"Whatever you do, don't say a thing, and don't make a whisper of a sound."

CHAPTER 23

The pirate captain moved in a clockwise path around the beach. About a quarter of a mile down the beach they found another path.

"This time you take Dirty, go check this out. And try not to get wet," warned the captain. In about half an hour, the captain stood up. "I have heard that before," he said, as a wall of water with four of his crew came down the side of the mountain. "I guess I should have sent some soap with you, Dirty," he said.

"I don't know what happened," said Dirty.

The captain looked at him with a priceless grin. "Now that would be a waterfall, I hope it was not too big of a shock for your system." Then he turned and walked away shaking his head. "It seems someone does not want us here. This is too much for the Squid to do." And they walked on. By the end of the day, the captain had lost track of how many times they had been washed down the side of a mountain. The only good thing at the very least, was for the first time in months, Dirty was clean, he thought. The pirate captain yelled at his men, "Back to the beach. Build a fire, that will be enough play time today."

As the sun went down in the west, again the sunset was like fire, only to be replaced with moonlight and breeze. As soon as the dark settled in, the screams began. This time there were many and they came from every direction.

"Captain, let's forget the squid and get off this island." All the crew was in favor of it.

"Now how would you propose to do that?" the captain asked. "We have no boat. And our island is just a little too far south to swim. But there has to be a boat on this island somewhere, even if it is a small one, even if we have to make one." said the captain. "Tomorrow, we start to build a raft."

"Then what?" asked one of the crew.

"Then we go home, either with the Squid or without him, and I will take my chances with Uncle Jamie." The captain knew he did not have a lot of choices.

The screams went on most of the night. The crew was more than jumpy. When morning came, they just wanted to rest. "Let's go!" grumbled the captain. "I have spent too many a night on this beach."

One of the men was walking far ahead and one was behind. They made their journey around the island.

The man in front yelled, "Captain, Squid is alive." The captain and the crew came running.

"Look beside that freshwater pool; it is Squid's shirt," said the crewman.

The captain picked the shirt up; he scouted around. "There are the boy's tracks and the sea dog. They are on the island. Fill up with fresh water. And let me think." The captain sat on a fallen palm tree. And the men went over for some fresh water. Two of his men were drinking out of the pool and one was filling his canteen. The rest of the men were down with the captain, not paying attention to the pond.

The ocean noise covered the sound of the first man to fall into the pool. Then the next. "What was that?" said the captain. He turned just when the last of the three hit the water. Captain LeDuval walked up to the edge of the pool. What was a peaceful pool of water was now bright red. "I think it will be a little safer if we stay on the beach. There is an island to the north; let us see if we can find anything that we can use to get off this island. The only other way off this island is to wait for a storm and cross when the sea is calm. We can't swim west until we pass the currents from between the islands, but for that, we will need a boat of some kind."

CHAPTER 24

Johnathan sat between Danny and Naughty. They ate some of the fruit and moss that they always had in their pouch. Johnathan watched his friends drape the moss over green and yellow fruit. When they did this, the fruit and moss blended in with whatever it touched. Johnathan covered the fruit with moss, the results were the same. When he separated the fruit from the moss, he could see them again.

Danny shook his head, "Now he knows that secret." And they waited and quietly watched. It was not long before they heard someone coming. Johnathan looked at Danny; he was already blending in with the jungle. Naughty put her hand on Johnathan. He could feel the warm sensation throughout his body. She was the perfect color with the jungle. Except for his shorts, he was also. Naughty quickly put some broadleaf over his shorts to cover them. They sat there and watched. First, the man came up and found the pool. He shouted for the captain. They all came running. The captain picked up Johnathan's shirt and pointed at the tracks.

He said, "The Squid is still alive." Then he went over and sat down as if to think of what to do next. Three of his men were next to the pond. Naughty put her hand over Johnathan's mouth. She knew what was going to happen. In an instant, all three were gone. The crew just stood next to the pond, which was now red. Johnathan's eyes were as big as the moon itself.

Naughty whispered in his ear, "You might want to close your eyes just a little." They sat there until the pirates had gone.

Danny looked at Naughty, "Well that went pretty well, I think." He looked at Johnathan, who watched the shocking end of the pirates.

"Those men were not very nice to me. One of them is the one that hit me in the face; they called him Smoll," Johnathan could not talk anymore.

Danny looked at Johnathan, "I don't think I have seen that side of you before."

Naughty grabbed Johnathan's hand as all three ran up the mountainside. "Tell me more about Smoll?" At the top of the mountain ridge they stopped, they could see the pirates going north.

Naughty looked Johnathan straight in the eyes. "Now, what about the Smoll, what did he do to you?"

Johnathan started to relive the encounters with the pirates. "Of all the pirates, he was the worst. He shot my friend, stole from my mother and father, and kidnapped me. If not for Captain LeDuval, he would have thrown me over the side of the ship." Johnathan put his arm around Hairy. "Isn't that right Hairy?" Johnathan just wanted to go home. Johnathan was crying now, "Where are you, Uncle Jamie." Naughty grabbed Johnathan and would not let him go until he was in control of his senses.

Danny watched as the boy relived his past with the pirates and said, trying to change the subject, "Naughty, if they want a boat so much, shouldn't we give them one?" said Danny.

"Why, what do you have in mind?" "You will see," said Danny.

At the flat place on top next to their stream around the island, Doggy jumped up and ran over to greet them with Tinker right behind. They had their own kind of sound, high pitched, but almost like live instruments moving up and down notes with movement of their trunks. Johnathan giggled when he saw them.

"Naughty, let's bring two canoes down to the beach; the last time we had visitors from the other island they left some; they were in a hurry to leave." Danny grinned.

"I could have them on the beach tonight. Then we will be done with the pirates. All day they watched the pirate crew walk around the island shore. They went clear to the north side of the island. The three could see them from outside of the cave.

"Johnathan, Naughty and I are going to get the canoes and take them down to the beach. If the pirates know what is best, they will go back to their own island." Johnathan watched Naughty and Danny go down the mountain. Hairy and Johnathan sat down and went to sleep. He dreamed about his Uncle Jamie, and where he could be, then he awoke almost in tears. If he only knew, his uncle was on the Pirate Island to the south.

CHAPTER 25

Jamie spent another day and night on the ship. No one had seen anything of the pirates. Everyone could feel the tension in the air. If the pirates were alive, they would be back. Jamie sent the small boat to shore for fresh fruit and water. "If you hear the gun, come back as soon as possible," he said. By the end of the day, most of the men had spent some time on shore.

The tension lessened. "Tomorrow should be a better day," Jamie thought.

CHAPTER 26

By nightfall, the pirates had made camp on the north side of the island. They could see the rocks and waves smashing over them from the east. There was no way they could leave that way. The captain sat next to the fire, "Tomorrow, we will go back the way we came." He still had Johnathan's shirt. "I wonder what happened to the little Squid. I kind of liked the little feller?"

"Captain, how do you think we are going to get off this island?" asked Dirty? I think the Devil himself lives here," said another of the crew.

"I think we will all see the devil in time, I don't know what is here, but I don't think it is the devil," said the captain. Just when all was quiet, the curdling screams started. That night they were everywhere in the jungle, and on the beach. It even seemed like the wind changed, even out at sea. The pirates stayed close to the fire all night.

CHAPTER 27

By morning Johnathan was outside the cave. Danny and Naughty were already sitting there. "Naughty, I thought you said you were the only one who could scream," Johnathan reminded her.

"No," Danny said, "only the lassies can scream like that."

"But last night, I heard screams everywhere. You were on the other side of the mountain. How did you do it?

"Johnathan, all in due time. Today we are going over to the other side of the island. We can see the Pirates' Bay from up there. So, let's get something to eat. Then we can go. Where is that Hairy dog of yours?" asked Naughty looking worried.

"Here he comes," Johnathan said. Hairy had a good run, his tail was wagging.

After eating fruit and moss, Danny said, "Would you like some meat?"

"I thought all you two ate was fruit and moss," Johnathan answered.

Danny looked back and said, "I told you that you did not know everything. Tell me, Johnathan, just what do you know about us?"

Johnathan stopped for a moment, "Well, you two act like brother and sister, not just friends. I really don't know how you got here, but I am sorry that your father and mother did not make it. How long has it been since you lost them? One thing that I know for sure is that if not for you two, I would not be here. You are my friends."

Naughty couldn't hold it much longer. She started to laugh. "Johnathan, we did not say that we lost our father and mother. Would you like to meet them?"

He looked at her surprised and said, "Yes."

They were off. They grabbed some broad leaves, and away they went. But this time only to stop on the east side of the mountains. Johnathan could see the waves crashing on the rocks. From where they were, he could see the thin beach go right to the jungle. The ocean was crystal clear light green. As if the sea was showing off its natural beauty of seaweed, reefs, and rocks. As Johnathan turned to the inside of the island, it was hidden by a valley blanketed by clouds. The clouds almost looked like a sea of white fog.

"Before we go any farther, you must tie this rope on Hairy," Naughty said. "Why? He has never had one on him before," Johnathan asked. "Johnathan, I will explain later, but for now please do what I ask."

Johnathan took the rope; it was made from vines. He called Hairy. "Come on, Hairy, let's put this on you."

"Put the rope over the top of his mouth then down, cross it under his mouth, and tie it behind his head. This will keep him from biting anything." Naughty said. Johnathan did as was asked; Hairy didn't seem to mind.

"We are ready," They started down the inside of the mountain. The clouds were so thick that Johnathan could hardly see where he was headed. Nevertheless, down they went. This time there was no pool to slip into, just a path down the mountainside.

Johnathan could not find it again if he had to. He told the two little people as they moved like lightning through the jungle. Then when he walked out into the clearing, he could not believe his eyes. There were goats and lambs. "Who takes care of them?" he asked.

"Just a little further, Johnathan, then you will see," Naughty looked at Johnathan and smiled.

He walked into the open area. Large trees grew up tickling the clouds. As he walked under the trees, he started to see some life. "In the top of the trees," He pointed, "Is that some kind of treehouse?" Naughty smiled; every tree had something built in it. There were wooden bridges from one tree to the other.

The sky was hidden, but the light shown through the clouds.

"Steps?" Johnathan asked as he looked at Naughty.

She pointed at the steps. “Before we go up, you must tie Hairy to the tree.” Johnathan tied Hairy to the tree just as he was asked. Then he climbed the steps all the way to the tops of the trees. As he reached the top, he could see house after house. It was like a city in the trees. But no one is at home. “Where is everyone?” he asked.

CHAPTER 28

Jamie looked at Pirate Bay. “We must have missed something. Let’s go back and look; there just has to be something.” Jamie and part of the crew went back to the beach. “Look around for anything. Fan out; we will meet you back here, and be careful,” Jamie smiled. “We have missed something.” The first thing Jamie did was go over to the area that had no beach. Overgrown, the dock was not visible until he was right next to it.

“Captain,” shouted one of the crew.

“Over here there are long boats.” Jamie came over to the boats.

“Don’t uncover them. Let’s see what else we can find,” said Jamie.

One of the other men yelled, “Captain, a cave!”

“Now we are getting somewhere. Don’t go into the cave till I get there,” commanded Jamie.

The cave had a little of everything. It looked like each time a ship would end up on the rocks, the pirate crew would take everything they could; food, gunpowder, and weapons.

“If the pirates are alive, they will be back. Take some of the gunpowder and put it on the mouth of the cave. Then take a small keg of powder and put one every few feet back in.” Jamie instructed his men. “Cover each one of them. But put something on it so we know where it is.”

“Now I need two men to hide next to the cave and wait. I want one pirate; I don’t care how you get him, but you get him.” warned Jamie. Two of the men waited on the shore. “They will not be here until dark; just get one. Do not let the rest know you are here.”

“Aye, aye, Captain.

“Back to the ship.”

CHAPTER 29

The pirates spent several restless hours on the beach. The ghostly screams went on most of the night, making everyone's taut nerves even more ragged and strained. The pirate captain started to walk back the way they had come. He did not say anything to the rest of the crew, but they followed him. By early morn, they had reached the area that had the freshwater pond. "Steer far from the pond. No need to feed the fish today," said the captain. As he looked at the jungle just ahead, there hidden next to the beach were two canoes. "This might just be our lucky day. Take the small boats back to the southern part of the beach," yelled the captain. The first mate got into one of the canoes. One of the other men got into the other. They took the canoes down the shoreline and waited for the captain.

"This is almost too easy." Captain LeDuval scratched his beard and lowered his eye. "Just before sunset, we will go back to our island. Build a big fire tonight, men, and by morning we will be back with the long boats." They could not all get in the small canoes. Each of the canoes had one side with outriggers to keep it from tipping. Even so, the men in the second canoe were in the water more than once. But by the time they reached the beach, they were doing very well considering all that had happened to them and the dead pirates. The captain watched with laughter as the two canoes went down the shoreline. We might have to put outriggers on both sides before this night is over," he said.

They made much better time at the beach than before. By the end of the day, they had rowed and marched to the southern part of the west beach. The men were out gathering wood for the fire; if they had learned anything, it was that they needed a good fire. The captain got into the canoe with his first mate behind him. Two other men were trying to get into the other canoe without tipping it over. The captain and the three men went out to sea. They went west past the swift water that ran between the islands, then turned south. It was just about dark when the pirates could see the bay. But there was a ship anchored in the mouth of the bay. Captain LeDuval put his hand out and in a very low voice; "Let us be very quiet, we will slip by the ship in the dark". They crossed the aft of the ship. The ocean was still like glass. The moon gave the sea light. The canoes glided right past Jamie's ship to the beach. Upon reaching the beach, the pirates hid the canoes. They went right for the long boats. "Be quiet, and let's get the boats to the beach. We have to move quickly; the night won't last forever," whispered Captain LeDuval. When the three boats were at the beach, the captain instructed, "Now let's make a fast trip to the cave." They went to the cave and got their weapons and powder. The captain took all the guns he could hold. The others did the same. When they got to the long boats, the captain looked around. He was missing one man. "Now where did he go? Start pushing the boats in the water. I will be right back." The captain went back to the cave but found no one. Now he ran back to the men. "Cast off, now," he whispered. They went right by the ship within twenty feet of the aft, then back to sea. The sun was just coming over the mountains as the three boats made it to the beach of the Island of the Shee. The fire was almost out. Most of the men were asleep but quickly awoke upon the captain's arrival. The captain rowed his boat to the beach. The other boats were right behind him.

"Captain, you are missing a man," said one of the crew with fear.

"Don't you think I know that? He yelled back. "I think the jungle got him." First, the bad news is Captain James is anchored in our bay. The good news is that we will have a ship by tomorrow. "Now let's eat and rest, for we have a big day coming," and with that the captain lay down in the sand, put his hat over his face, and went to sleep.

CHAPTER 30

Johnathan stopped at the top of the steps. "No one in sight, where is everyone?" he asked.

Naughty took his hand, "Follow me," she trilled. They walked past many small huts. Johnathan didn't think he could get through the doors. Up ahead a large area opened. There was a fire built in the center of the area. The fire had sand and rocks all around it. In the center of the fire was food cooking on a spit, and a pot of something, too.

"Where is everyone?" he asked.

"So, this is Johnathan. He is rather big for a boy," commented a voice out of nowhere.

"Johnathan, please sit down; there is something we would like to show you," said Naughty. He sat down slowly on the wood floor. He could see in every direction one little hut after another. Each hut was made from materials from the jungle. There were even handrails from tree branches.

"Johnathan, this is my mother Keavy and this is my father Cahir," said Naughty. Johnathan looked at the place where the voice came from; two little people appeared right before his confused eyes.

Keavy was not as tall as Naughty or Danny, but she had a sweet smile, and then Keavy said, "Welcome, Johnathan."

Cahir was a little taller, and he did not smile. Keavy said, "Cahir, try to look just a wee bit friendlier. We don't get many visitors here. Let us make him feel at home." Cahir just walked away shaking his head.

Naughty said, "Johnathan, father remembers what the people did to us in the old land, Juverna." (Ireland)

"What did they do?" asked Johnathan.

"We are small, they are big. They hunt anything that they don't understand. They even use dogs or Conans (wolf or hound) to find us," Naughty said.

"Is that why Harry was tied up?" Johnathan asked.

"Yes, at our home in Juverna, we were hunted and feared. We have traveled all over the world. We have people almost everywhere. But it is always the same."

"Where are the rest of your people?" asked Johnathan.

Keavy raised her arm and waved. Then she said, "Now make yourself known to Johnathan." As he watched, Johnathan could see little people everywhere. They all waved at him, smiled, and went on their way. They were right by him all the time.

"Johnathan, would you like something to eat?" Keavy pointed at a table. Then she laughed, "That won't do, I'm afraid that you are too big."

"Naughtia, would you get something for Johnathan to sit on?" she said. Naughty smiled and nodded her head yes.

Keavy looked at Johnathan, "Now tell me, Johnathan, how did you get here?

Johnathan told the story about the pirates, and Uncle Jamie coming to get him.

"What does Uncle Jamie's ship look like?" asked Keavy.

"It is just about the best ship in the world. A lot better than the ship the pirates had," he enthusiastically responded.

"After eating, Danny and Naughty, would you take Johnathan up to the southwest side of the island and show him the pirate's bay. A ship waits just outside of the bay and looked as if it was war-familiar. Maybe it is Uncle Jamie's." But for now, we eat," said Keavy. Johnathan sat on a pillow that Naughty gave him. There was roasted lamb, potatoes and milk, everything you could think of even melon for dessert."

"Uncle Jamie told me about fireflies. They are everywhere." Keavy, directed Johnathan to watch." She held up her hands to the small lights. They immediately swarmed over to her. "Now look closely at our fragile friends." Johnathan held out his hand. One of the fairies landed on it. She was trying to say something. Johnathan carefully raised the fairy to his ear.

"Hello, Johnathan, pleased to meet you," she sang quietly. Johnathan gently lowered his hand, and she flew away.

"This is why your dog must be tied and not allowed to bite," Keavy admonished.

Danny came over to Johnathan, "We must go over to the other side of the island, are you ready?"

"Yes," said Johnathan, wondering why."

Down the steps they went; Hairy was ready. He had a bowl of water and was chewing on a bone. There were little people watching the sheep and goats. They all waved as the boy and dog went up the inside of the mountain. They came out right in the same spot that they came in. "This was the best part of the island," thought Johnathan. They grabbed some broad leaves and away they went in the stream. Each time that Johnathan though he was going to stop, water from out of the ground shot him up, and they started again. Soon they were at the southwest side of the island.

"Come on, Johnathan," said Danny sternly, "this way."

The ocean was visible to the west and the island to the south and the white coral sand around the island. The ocean was flowing very fast between the two islands. "Is that your uncle's ship?" He looked as hard as he could; then he saw Uncle Jamie's flag, a dove holding a cannon and felt a thrill of relief and love flow through his whole being.

"That is his ship! The Fighting Dove, Uncle Jamie is here." Johnathan almost cried.

"We'll need to hurry! We must go to the beach to tell the others. I wonder where the pirates are?" Danny mused to himself. This time they went all the way around the island, what a ride! Even Hairy was tired. When they got back to the trees, Johnathan tied up Hairy, and ran up the steps. Cahir and Keavy sat waiting for them.

Cahir put out his hand, "Johnathan, the pirates are going to attack the ship. Is that your uncle's ship?"

"Yes!" yelled Johnathan.

"We must give your uncle a hand then." And with that Cahir turned and walked away.

Naughty looked at Johnathan. She could see that he was worried. "Johnathan, Cahir is over three hundred years old. He has been in many battles. Your uncle is in good hands."

"How could anyone be that old?" Johnathan asked.

"As we told you, there are many things that you don't know. How old do you think Danny and I are?" asked Naughty.

"I don't know," shrugged Johnathan.

"Danny and I are almost fifty years old. Now let's us see what Cahir wants us to do." They walked over to the big area between the tree huts. There are many little people sitting around. All were talking at once.

Then Keavy stood up. "We are not going to get anything done if you don't stop your bickering. Cahir, what do you have in mind?"

"Danny and Naughty have Doggy and Tinker on the shoreline at dark. Talk to the others; we want as many elephants and riders as we can find with rocks and slings. Tonight, the Banshee will strike. We have let these pirates go too long, now we strike." Johnathan sat there watching the little people form up like an army, each one knowing what to do, each one was ready. He was itching to be part of this. Johnathan could hear a noise like a huge fan above his head in the clouds. As he watched, two small dragons came into view.

"Are those dragons?" asked Johnathan.

"Yes, Johnathan," replied Keavy. They were here when our people came to this island. They are both males; one is a little smarter than the other. Now watch and you will see what I mean." The first dragon came down very gracefully, but the second came with a thud and a bounce. Both were smiling as they walked over to Johnathan.

"They are not very big; I thought dragons were bigger?" mused Johnathan.

"Don't know, these are the only dragons we have seen," replied Naughty. "Now watch; they both eat as much of the jungle as they can hold, they eat just about anything. Then they start to swell up with gas. (methane) and get bigger. Now watch Johnathan, with a little help from their wings, they rise up into the air. Aed, is the smart one. We named him after our ancestors. He takes care of Aga." After a rough landing, Aga came over and smelled Johnathan. "Aga, can't control his burping or gas very much. When he has too much gas inside him, he starts to rise up into the air. Their wings don't move very fast.

His breath smells like rotten eggs." replied Johnathan.

"His wings don't have to move fast, now watch Johnathan. "When Aed beaths fire, each time that he does he goes lower. Aga, never learned how to breathe fire. He waits for Aed, to help him out a little. His way of getting rid of his gas is different, watch."

Johnathan watched; the second dragon, Aga, kept rising until they heard a loud passing of the wind. When Aga passed wind, Aed set the wind on fire. The dragon shot through the sky like a cannon, his head reaching around looking at the back of him to see what the noise was. Then he glided back to the ground. Aed, had a very mischievous grin on his face. Aed, glided down near Johnathan.

"His name is Aed, Aed means Fire," reasoned Danny. Next the second dragon came down with a not so smooth landing, almost sliding into a tree. "Sometimes we call Aga, Albatross for his crash landings," replied Naughty.

Johnathan was almost starting to laugh when Keavy came up to him. "Johnathan, there is one thing. You must promise you will never tell anyone one about what you have seen here. We have friends all over the world. Their safety is in your hands, do you understand?"

"Yes, I understand," he promised.

Naughty and Johnathan walked back to the steps. "Naughty, how do you blend in so I can't see you?" asked Johnathan.

"Johnathan, we brought crops from Juverna, the moss and fruit. When you eat them together, you can do a lot of things. But for now, we must get ready for the battle."

"Do you mean to change so I can't see you" Johnathan asked.

"Yes, Johnathan," answered Naughty. "We have become invisible as far back as anyone can remember."

CHAPTER 31

The last pirate came out of the cave in the inky shadows of the moonlight. Before he knew what hit him, the two men grabbed him and put a knife to his throat. Then before he could say anything he was gagged and bound. They all sat in the darkness until the rest of the pirates had left the shore.

Jamie watched the three pirate boats go past the ship. He ordered the men to stay out of sight. "They will be coming back tomorrow night to take the ship. But we won't be here," Jamie said slyly.

Jamie was waiting at the rail when his crew brought the captured pirate back to the ship.

"Well, look what we have here. Bring him to my quarters. Did anyone see you?"

"No, sir, they didn't seem to care if they lost this one or not," said the crewmen in disgust.

They walked across the deck, Jamie turned toward the crewmen, "We will be leaving at daybreak. All hands be ready." Jamie walked into the cabin scowling at the prisoner. "Now tell me, is my nephew still alive?" Jamie looked right in the eyes of the captured pirate. The pirate was sweating and shaking. Jamie said, "Don't make me ask again."

"We haven't seen him since we shipwrecked on the island. We found his shirt and saw his footprints in the sand. But I haven't seen him since." The pirate knew this was not the time to stop talking.

"Where are the rest of the pirates?" Jamie had the prisoner by the neck.

"Just on the other side of the fast water that flows between the islands; they are on the beach." By this time the pirate's face was turning blue.

"Take him below and put him in chains. We will deal with him later." Jamie walked out on the deck. His crew gathered around.

It did not take long. The crew were all standing around Jamie. "The pirates will be back tonight. But we will have a surprise for them. Master of Arms, can you hit the powder in front of the cave-and blow that keg into the sky?"

"Aye, aye, sir," he said.

"Good. Before we leave this morning, make sure you know exactly where it is; you might have to hit it at night, and can you do it?"

"Aye, aye sir."

"Good, you two men go back to the island. We will be anchored out of sight. When you see them return, you let me know," insisted Jamie.

"How do you want us to let you know?"

"Two shots from the south side of the mountain; that way the pirates cannot hear you. If you see Johnathan, fire three shots." Jamie looked at the two men. "Do you understand?"

"Yes, sir," they answered back.

"Over the side then and be careful." Jamie walked over to the side as the men left for the shore. "Pull up the anchor; we are going to sea." And Jamie went to the helm. "We are headed southwest, but we will be back in a few hours."

CHAPTER 32

Things were getting very busy. All the little people were getting ready for the battle. It looked like they had done this before. One by one, they went up the side of the mountain and out of sight. When Johnathan, Naughty, and Danny got to the top, Tinker and Doggy were there. They were glad to see them. They raised their front feet then their back all the while turning a circle, apparently doing a happy dance.

"Johnathan, look at their feet; you can see they have web feet; just the thing for swimming, wouldn't you say?" asked Naughty.

Naughty and Danny each had knives in their belts. "We are ready; let's go. Let's give them a proper send-off." Naughty grabbed some broad leaves, and they all went on the water ride around the crater. When they reached the spot overlooking the pirates, they stopped. "We wait until dark; then the first thing that we do is, scare them right into the sea," Naughty whispered.

"Johnathan, you and Hairy stay in the jungle. This is no place for you, so sit and watch." Danny ordered as he started down the mountain toward the pirates.

"Now, whatever you do, don't move, or say anything. We have asked some friends to stay with you until we get back."

"What kind of friends?" asked Johnathan. Johnathan looked at his shoulder; sitting on his left shoulder was a little fairy.

"Johnathan, if you are very quiet, she will talk to you," said Naughty.

"Are you a fairy?" asked Johnathan.

"Yes, Johnathan, we will be with you until it is safe to go home." The fairy pointed to the beach.

"There must be hundreds of little people here," said Johnathan. They were ready to strike. Cahir was giving the orders now; Johnathan sat with Hairy and the fairy and watched. The sky was dark blue; the ocean glittered with even a darker shade of blue. The sun had not yet set. Cahir raised his hand then dropped it. The battle was on. All the lasses started screaming. They came from every direction at once. Then all the men started running down to the beach.

CHAPTER 33

The pirates rested all morning. But by noon they were all business and ready for action. All the boats were packed full of weapons and powder and anything else that they could use to take Jamie's ship. The quietness lasted until the sun was almost setting. Just before dusk the screaming started-but different this time. Before, it was a warning. Now, it was the scream of death itself approaching. On both sides of the beach, the perplexed combatants could see dust from the sand coming closer, but still, no one was in sight. The pirates stood and watched as the sandstorm came closer. They could not see what was making the storm. This utterly confused them.

Then, Captain LeDuval yelled! "Into the boats. It's now or never."

Everyone went running for the sea. All fifty men ran for the boats. The sound of death was almost on top of them. The first boat with the captain went to sea, with the second one right behind. Before the third boat could get off, the Shee attacked. The high pitch shrill sound was all around them. The men were swinging their swords and stabbing the air. When one pirate would pause to see what he was fighting, he was dragged back to the beach and quickly neutralized. He lay lifeless, never knowing what had happened. The third boat got about one hundred feet from the shore. Danny and Naughty were right next to the boat. Tinker and Doggy had their trunks waving in the air above the surface of the sea. The only thing that was seen was a water shadow of their trunks. Tinker slashed his trunk across the chest of one of the pirates. Over the side he went. Doggy did the same on the other side while the other little people rocked the boat just for fun. All the men in that boat were screaming. One of the men started swinging his oar. All they could hear was laughing and screaming. "What kind of demons are these Shee?" The boat rocked back and forth from the men swinging at the air and the little people rocking the craft. While swinging the oar, the pirate caught one of his shipmates right on the side of his head. Over the side he went, like his other poor losers.

"Naughty, sharks!" called Danny. "Let's get back to the shore." The water around the boat was red from the loss of a few pirates and started a feeding frenzy with the sharks. The water around the boat was foaming in the moonlight from the sharks enjoying a tasty meal. The men in the boats just kept rowing and left the men in the feeding frenzy to fend for themselves. Then all was quiet except the echoed screams from the Shee on the shore, but not close to the boat. Now it was about dark. The pirates regrouped out at sea.

"How many did you lose?" asked the captain.

One of the men raised his hand, with four fingers up. "This place is truly a place of demons," he groaned.

Then one of the men said, "Captain, do you hear what I hear?"

The captain was quiet. He held his hand up, as if to call for quiet. Then he smiled, "It is the sea dog." Then he took out his glass and looked at the beach. In the moonlight he could see Johnathan. "Well, the Squid made it. Let's stay out here for a while longer. After we get our new ship, we will come back for Squid. It would seem that he has become friends with the Shee." With that, the captain scratched his beard and motioned with his head to go.

They drifted for a while. One of the crew said, "Look, Captain, look at The Island of the Shee."

"The island looks like it is on fire. The inside of the island must be a volcano," said the captain. The sky above the island glowed with orange light on the bottom of the clouds, flickering in the moonlight.

As the boat went out of sight, all they could hear was, "Squid made friends with the Shee."

The pirates rowed the rest of the night. Early morning, they could see the bay. "Careful now," said the captain. Uncle Jamie should be right around the corner. Stick to the shoreline and keep her close." Slowly they reached the mouth of the bay.

"Captain, there is no ship," called the crewman.

"Don't you think that I know it," answered the captain. "Now where could Uncle Jamie be? Just keep rowing and take us over to the dock. We will check that cave."

CHAPTER 34

Jamie's men watched from the top of the mountain. Just about daybreak three boats were on the horizon. They watched as the pirates came to the bay. As soon as they passed the mouth of the bay, one of Jamie's men went over to the south side of the mountain. "There was Jamie's ship." He shot two times in the air. He watched as the sails went up. The ship was on its way. Then he went back to the other man, and they watched as the boats went across the bay to the dock.

Jamie yelled, "All hands, this time it is for real. When we get close enough for a shot, I want that cave blown away." The crew had all the cannons on the starboard side ready.

"Before we fire, make sure Johnathan is not with the pirates, understand." "Aye, aye," answered the crew. Jamie knew he did not have to tell the crew to watch for Johnathan. "What a morning," thought Jamie, "blue sea, white cotton clouds in the sky, and the perfect wind. Not too much and not too little." It did not take long to reach the mouth of the bay. Like a ghost ship, they glided right into the bay. The crew was careful not to make a sound. Jamie watched the shore. The pirates didn't see them coming.

Jamie walked over to the cannons, "When you know you can make the shot, fire at will."

"Aye, sir," said the men.

"A little further, let the ship swing around."

"Fire!" The morning was awakened by the earthshattering boom of the big guns. Just as the guns went off, the cave exploded, while the pirates flew like leaves in the wind. The crew were already lowering the boats. They were ready to do the job that was ahead of them. Like clockwork, they hit the beach. If there were any pirates still on their feet, they could not be seen.

Jamie yelled, “See if any of them are still alive and bring them to me.” “Over here, captain, these two are still alive.”

Jamie walked over to the men. Both men were injured; one was hurt badly.

“Where is my nephew?” Jamie ordered. “Tell me before I run you though with my sword.”

Both pirates hastily answered at the same time, “The Shee have him. He was on the beach last night. We were attacked by the Shee. The boy and his dog were on the beach.”

“Johnathan does not have a dog,” Jamie said. “If you know what is in your best interest, you will tell me the truth.”

“Captain! We are telling you the truth. The Shee have the boy.”

“Take them back to the ship. We will deal with them later.” Jamie told the crew men. “And see if there are any signs of the rest of the scum.” Then Jamie went back to the boats.

CHAPTER 35

Johnathan walked down to the beach staying out of sight, first hearing the screams. The trilling shrieks came from all sides of the beach. Then the pirates could hear the feet running on the sand. As they came closer, he could hear them also. Hundreds of feet running towards the pirates. Tinker and Doggy were having much too good a time. The pirates were swinging blindly in fear of what they could not possibly understand. The elephants were playing a very dangerous game, as were all the Shee. In a panic, the pirates made a break for their boats. Johnathan thought that was the quickest he had ever seen the pirates move. Captain LeDuval was the first one to reach the boats, pushing off like a coward even before all the crew were aboard. Johnathan was giggling to himself as he watched the pirate crew tripping, falling over and yelling at one another.

The first boat was off. The captain was yelling at the men. “Faster, faster.” Then he grabbed one of the oars away from one of the men and started to row himself.

The second boat hit the water right after the first. But the third did not make it. The footprints in the sand were right next to the boat. As the men got knocked down. Johnathan saw one of the men get hit right across the face. He knew it had to be Tinker. He could hear the small elephants making themselves known, their powerful trunks slamming into the crew. At least three or four of the pirates had fallen over the side of the boat. The rest of the pirates kept rowing, not stopping to look back.

The Caribbean Sea was roiling foam and white water. Johnathan saw the splashing in the moonlight and knew he had seen this frenzy before. Then came the screams, not from the Shee, but from the men who were in the water. Then as fast as it started it was over. The boy could see the footprints coming out of the water, not wanting to tangle with the sharks.

Cahir called back to the village, "It will be a long time before the pirates come back to this shore."

Hairy started barking when the Shee came back on the beach. Johnathan could not hold him; the dog ran down to the beach, with Johnathan right after him.

When he caught Hairy, he was with Naughty and Danny. All that could be seen were their shadows.

"Johnathan! Get off the beach; they will see you," said Naughty.

Johnathan turned and ran back to the jungle edge with Hairy right behind him. Up the path on the mountain, the Shee went. The Shee were excited. When they got to the top of the mountain, torches were lit next to the stream, out of sight from the shore, where piles of large broad leaves were placed for their return. They took the leaves and sledded off. This time was better than ever. Riding the stream in the dark by the light of the moon and torches was exhilarating. It is a good thing Naughty and Danny were in front; Johnathon could see only moonlight and jungle. This time they stopped at a different place. How could the Shee tell where they were? It all looked the same to Johnathan. He looked at the clouds in the center of the island; they looked like they were on fire, with an orange glow, bright at the bottom and lighter at the top.

Danny instructed, "Johnathan, this way." They walked down the inside of the mountain, more torches lighting the way.

Johnathan stood with his mouth open. "I have never seen anything like this before. This is beautiful." He was in a daze.

Naughty took his hand; "Come on Johnathan, everyone is waiting." She started to run. Johnathan could hardly keep up. How could anyone so small go so fast? The tree huts were glowing. The village in the trees lit up the clouds above them. This was the most beautiful and mystic place that Johnathan had ever seen. They were at the steps to the tree huts. Johnathan tied Harry up, and up they went. At the top of the steps were hundreds of little people. They were enjoying a victory celebration.

"We don't get to run the pirates off very often," said Keavy.

"Come, Johnathan, and sit with us."

Keavy smiled at Johnathan, "We have wanted to chase the pirates away for a long time. Finally, it is done." Keavy was peering at Johnathan with an affectionate gaze.

"Do think they are gone for good?" asked Johnathan. "Captain LeDuval seems a lot smarter than the rest of them. He does not give up very easily."

"Now, Johnathan, don't worry about the pirates. Now we must find a way to get you back to your uncle." Keavy and Cahir nodded their heads as if they were trying to formulate a plan together.

"Johnathan, would you stand up with me?" asked Keavy.

"Just as I thought; you are just a wee bit taller than you were when you came to us. Before long you will be much too big for this island. We must get you back to your uncle. They all sat around the fire in the open area in the tree huts. There was plenty of food and drink. Some of the little people were acting really silly.

They were dancing and singing to weird music. Some of the little people were playing their fiddles. Johnathan was getting tired, even with the loud music, and soon he gave way to sleep. The next morning, he awoke in the trees, close to the fire. Someone had covered him with blankets.

"Good morning to you, Johnathan," said Keavy. "Did you sleep well?" "Yes, but where is everyone?"

"Each one of us has things to do. We have to be ready for unforeseen events."

"Like pirates?" Johnathan guessed

"Yes, even pirates," answered Keavy. "Johnathan, Cahir and I have come up with a plan. As soon as you have eaten, Danny and Naughty will take you down to the beach. They will help you build a fire on the southwest side of the beach. Then when your uncle comes, he will see you. Then he will send a boat and take you home. And, Johnathan, remember that you can't tell anyone what you have seen here. Do I have your word on it?"

“Yes, Keavy, you can trust me, I will not tell anyone about the island or the people here. Keavy, will I ever see you again?” Johnathan started to cry.

She grabbed Johnathan, “Our people are everywhere. So, it is always possible. But it is too dangerous for you to come back here.” She appeared to be sad to see him go. Danny and Naughty sat down, and they ate their last meal together. No one said anything. It was a very quiet meal, but one that Johnathan would never forget.

“Johnathan, I will miss you,” said Naughty.

“And I,” said Danny. “Even your dog, Hairy. Hurry now, we will not want to miss Uncle Jamie.”

Johnathan looked up and smiled, “I’m ready, let’s go.”

Keavy walked up to Johnathan, “Johnathan, when you came to us you were just a scared little boy. You have seen more than most have in a lifetime. As you go back, you go back as a young man. Your family will be very proud of you. And I will miss you, Johnathan James.”

“Looks like Mother is going to cry again,” said Danny.

They went down from the city of tree huts. Then they went up the inside of the mountain for the last time. Johnathan knew that he would miss the rides on the stream.

“This is the last time I will ride the stream; I will miss you two.” Johnathan’s tears were starting to show. The three reached the top. As Johnathan gathered the broad leaf for his last ride, he could see Naughty; she had tears streaming down from her sad eyes. She quickly disappeared, then reappeared after she had dried her checks.

“I will miss you, Johnathan,” she said, with a trembling lower lip. They slid down to the beach. Danny and Tinker already had some wood for a fire. Naughty and Johnathan went for some more. It was not long before they had a fire going. Danny put some wet grass on the fire so it would give off some smoke.

Then they waited for Uncle Jamie.

CHAPTER 36

About half of the pirates were in the cave. The captain was looking around. “There is something not right. Someone has been in the cave. There is some powder missing! You men look and see where it is.” Before they could move, the cannons on The Fighting Dove opened fire.

Captain Jamie James yelled, “Fire again.” The entrance to the cave was gone.

“Light some torches, you misfits,” Yelled LeDuval. The pitch black soon was torch bright. “Be careful to stay away from the powder. And follow me,” cried the captain. The shaken crew slinked to the back of the cave, right behind LeDuval. A breeze pulled the smoke off the torches. “Follow the smoke and see where it leads us.” Up ahead of the men, the sound of running water grew audible. As the pirates got closer, they could see a pool, and they could see an eerie light under the water.

Captain LeDuval said, “Tie a rope to me, and if you feel me pull on it, yank me back.” The men seemed relieved that he was going and not them.

Into the pool he went. The captain dived under the water. He held his breath for only a short time; then he came up on the outside the cave. He climbed out onto the bank and tied the rope to a tree. He made sure it was secure and dived back into the pool. When he surfaced at the inside of the pool, he watched his men stare at him.

“The Devil made it,” yelled one of the startled men.

“Well, what are you waiting for. Follow the rope and pull your miserable selves up the other side.” One by one the men jumped into the pool. And, one by one they made it to the other side. This time they were clear of the cave.

Captain LeDuval was the last to come out of the water. He looked at one of the men. "Go and see where we are. Don't let James see you. We must have spent the most part of the day getting out of the cave." The man took off running.

Soon he returned. "Captain, we are on the other side of the bay. We are close to the boats."

"Good, let's get to the boats. We are going to offer Squid a boat ride."

LeDuval could tell that the crew was not happy about going back to the Island of the Shee. "Now if we want to get old Uncle Jamie's ship, we have to have some bargaining power. And Squid is all we need."

The pirates moved through the jungle, careful not to make any noise. They slowly removed their boats from the beach and were headed for the open sea. All they had to do was catch the stream from between the two islands and follow it out to sea. The current was fast when they reached the stream. They had to steer

carefully away from the rocks. After riding the current out, they turned north up the coast. As they looked at the island, they could see smoke on the beach. The captain took out his looking glass. He looked once, then again. He set the glass down. "I don't think I believe my eyes." He wiped the glass clean. And looked again. "Here," he said, look through this glass. The captain handed it to the first mate. "What do you see?"

"I see Squid and his dog sitting on the beach," said the first mate.

"Did you see anything else?" The captain asked as he tilted his head and scratched his beard.

"No, sir, nothing else," he answered.

The captain, still rubbing his beard, "I thought I saw two people sitting with Squid. They were not very big. Let's get to the beach and fetch the boy. Now row hard." The captain had seen something, but he did not know what it was.

CHAPTER 37

Jamie was checking out the bay for any signs of life.

"Captain," yelled the look-out from The Fighting Dove. "Look over to the other side of the bay. Some of the pirates have made it to the boats. And they are headed out to sea."

Jamie shouted back to the ship. "Are they heading back to the Island of the Shee?"

Jamie's crew scrambled back to the ship. "Hoist the sails, let's get this ship out to sea. The anchor was already up. As soon as The Fighting Dove came around, Jamie commanded, "Fire." By this time the pirates were way ahead of the ship. But the chase was on. The pirates were almost out of sight. But Jamie's ship was gaining on them. Jamie took the ship directly west until they cleared the fast stream and the rocks right into the blue water. "Turn the ship north and have the cannons ready." As the ship went north, Jamie could see smoke and a fire on the beach. There was Johnathan. He was waving and jumping up and down. Jamie looked again; Johnathan had a large dog with him.

The pirates were headed for Johnathan. "Open fire on the boats, don't let them get close to Johnathan."

"Open fire now!" Jamie loudly directed. The cannons roared. All round the boats the cannonballs fell, but not one of them hit their target. Jamie watched as the pirates got to the beach. He saw Johnathan run into the jungle. But the dog stayed and fought. The dog attacked the pirates. But there were too many of them. Some of the men caught Johnathan. He was kicking them, but it was of no use. Jamie just watched in horror; he had come too far to be stopped now. Jamie ordered the ship to get as close as possible to the island. They dropped anchor and waited.

They waited for some kind of break; however, he had no plan at this time.

CHAPTER 38

Danny watched the pirates come on shore. Naughty went back to the tree village. When Naughty arrived at the village, Cahir was waiting. They had been watching the beach from on top of the mountain.

"Tonight, we will make another trip to the beach. This time we will end the pirates' fight forever," the older man promised.

Keavy looked worried, "Do you think they will hurt Johnathan"?

"No," Cahir said. "He is the only thing keeping them alive. Johnathan is safe for now. But tonight, this will end. I want everyone on the beach. We will chase the pirates into the sea for the last time. They will not touch land again. We will attack by the moonlight," said Cahir.

"Will Johnathan know what to do?" asked Naughty.

"He has no choice; he has to do the right thing. Naughty, I want you to go up to Johnathan. Cut his ropes. When the time is right, tell him to jump on Doggy's back with you." Cahir put his hand on Naughty's hand. "We will save the boy. I know how much he means to you."

"I even like him myself, but don't tell Keavy." Naughty smiled as she gave Cahir a hug. "Thank you, father."

"Now let's get everything we need down to the beach." And Cahir walked away, giving orders to the rest of the Shee.

CHAPTER 39

Captain LeDuval had Johnathan tied up and kept him close to the fire.

"Captain, the Shee, they will be here before too long. It is almost dark." Whined a seriously frightened pirate whose brave and swaggering front was slipping.

"Let me worry about the Shee," said Captain LeDuval. "I think that I will go see Uncle Jamie." With that he took a crew member and got into one of the boats and was rowed out to the ship. The Fighting Dove was five hundred yards out. "Captain Jamie James," the pirate called out. "Can you hear me." The pirate was waving a white flag.

"I hear you, what do you want?" Jamie demanded.

"Well, we seemed to have gotten off to a bad start. I would like to make you an offer," yelled LeDuval, in a smooth and easy tone of voice as he smiled and rubbed his beard. He would not look Jamie in the face, but out of the side of his eye.

Jamie watched as the pirate came closer. "I don't trust that one. He would kill us all if he could."

"What is your offer?" demanded Jamie.

"As soon as the darkness sits in, the Shee on will come screaming." said the pirate.

"And," said Jamie.

"So how would you like to give us poor humble sailors a lift off the island? And in return, we could deliver that fine boy back to his uncle."

"Jamie looked right at the captain, "The only way you will come on my ship is in chains. Here is what I will do for you. First, go back and get my nephew. Bring him back here. When he is on my ship, without one scratch. I will leave you on the island. You can leave and go back to your Pirate Island or stay. The choice is yours. How fast can you get back to the shore?" Jamie grabbed a rifle from one of the men.

Captain LeDuval answered, "You would not fire on the white flag, now would you!"

Jamie yelled, "I just want you to go back as fast as you can." Then Jamie took sight of the long boat. He carefully put a hole in the boat just below the water line. "This conversation is over. If I were you, Captain, I would get back, as soon as possible? I have heard that there are sharks in this part of the sea."

LeDuval looked at the small hole in the boat. Then they started to row, as fast as they could to the shore, there was no need to be ordered. He kept looking back, just to see that Jamie was not going to take another shot. All the while he was saying some not very nice things back to the ship that, fortunately, Captain Jamie could not hear for the slap of the oars.

On the south side of the beach, down from the pirates, were hundreds of the Shee just off the sand at the edge of the jungle. Elephants and riders-the lasses and lads were everywhere waiting with anticipation for the sun to go down. Some were on foot and some on the elephants. On the north side of the beach were also hundreds of Shee just waiting for Cahir to give the word to charge.

Naughty blended in with the beach, as only a shadow. She went right up to Johnathan. She whispered, "Johnathan, are you alright?"

He smiled and shook his head. "I knew you would be here."

"Johnathan, I will cut your ropes. But do not move. When the time is right you will jump on Doggy's back with me. Then we will drive the outlaws into the sea, then attack. Will you be alright?"

Johnathan smiled and nodded his head but did not say anything. Naughty went back to her elephant and waited.

A small pass going out to the beach was crowded, for Cahir and many of the little people were lined up ready for the charge. There were two large rocks on each side of the pass. Cahir was waiting for the right time. The sun was almost retired for the day. It wouldn't be much longer. Danny and the rest were ready. The blue sky was starting to go light purple. The ocean was going from dark blue to light green. And the tide was coming in. The moon was just coming up in the sky.

Captain LeDuval was close to the shore. "Get out here and help me get this boat to shore." When his men looked, the boat was almost full of water. The captain was sitting in sea water up to his sword.

"Captain, your boat must have sprung a leak!" said one of the crew.

The captain just looked at him, "Do you really think so. Maybe it has something to do with the gunshot in the side of the boat. One of you men patch that hole. We will need this boat in a very short while." The captain stepped out of the boat. All of his men moved out of his way.

He walked over to Johnathan. "Well, Squid," said the captain. "It seems that your uncle would like to see you. I hope that you have enjoyed our time together. Would you give your uncle my best? It has been a pleasure to meet you." He put on a fake smile and walked away.

"Captain," asked one of the pirates. "We are not going to just give Squid back, are we?"

"What do you think? The only way we are going to get off this island is to take Jamie's ship. "Now, let us go back to the fire." And the captain walked away.

The pirates had a large fire going at the beach. Johnathan was on the east side of the fire. Just off to the side of the jungle. The captain and his men, sat on the west side of the fire. The captain took a stick. He started to draw some lines in the sand. We have three boats, and we can all get in the boats. As soon as it is dark enough, we take the boats and go around to the port side of Jamie's ship. Do not make any noise. And the men will be watching me with the boy. When we get close enough to the ship, the men from the other two boats will scale the port side of the ship. Kill everyone who gets in your way. I will take Squid next to the ship with a pistol pointed right at his head. No one will see you come aboard. We will take the ship and leave Jamie and his men to the Shee. I told you that the boy would be useful." The captain looked at the other side of the fire where Johnathan was.

But Johnathan was gone. The pirates ran to the other side of the fire to look for the boy who had just disappeared. "It will be dark soon captain, what will we do. The Shee will be here anytime."

Captain LeDuval looked around. "Uncle Jamie does not know we don't have him. Same plan. Get anything you can and put it in that blanket; make it look like a boy in it. Uncle Jamie will not know until it is too late."

CHAPTER 40

Naughty watched as the pirate captain came ashore. His boat was full of water. She laughed to herself. Then all the pirates went over to the other side of the fire to see the wet captain.

When they were not looking, she ran over to Johnathan. “Come on, Johnathan,” she grabbed his hand and took him into the jungle. “Are you alright” she asked.

“Yes, then he grabbed her and gave her hug. “I am so glad to see you.” Naughty took Johnathan to Cahir, who was waiting at the edge of the jungle.

“The sky is almost dark, and there are clouds coming in. We can use this to our advantage,” said Cahir. “All they will see is the shadows of us coming after them. We must drive them into the sea!” He looked at Naughty, “Scream, now is the time!”

Naughty screamed then someone else screamed. In an instant, there were hundreds of screams coming from the north, the south, and the jungle.

All the pirates jumped to their feet. “To the boats, men!” yelped the captain.

Jamie had been watching the shore. He watched the captain get back to the beach. He saw them tie Johnathan up on the other side of the fire. But as the fire became larger, he could not see Johnathan.

Then in the sky above the beach, a small fire-breathing dragon arose. Then another one. The second one was rising higher and higher. The first one breathed fire right behind the second one. It lit up the sky with fire right behind him as he swooped down on the beach.

“Something must be going on. All the pirates rushed to the other side of the fire,” said Jamie. The next thing that he could see was what looked like someone was tied up inside of a blanket. "If they hurt Johnathan," Jamie threatened.

The first mate looked at Jamie, "I know sir, I know."

Then as the sun went down the pirates started running for the boats. The pirates had the bundle on their backs. They threw the bundle in the bottom of the boat. There was no movement. Jamie hands clutched the rail in anger. He watched as the boat left the shore. The other two boats were not far from the first. "All hands prepare for anything. Keep an eye on the other two boats," said Jamie.

The clouds were driving in fast, blocking the moon. Jamie looked at the first mate, and realized that if ever moonlight was essential, this was the night. By now Jamie could hear the screams. They were coming from everywhere. He remembered the sound from his last visit to the island. All he could do was stay right where he was and wait. All the screams seem to be getting louder as if they were coming out to sea. On the beach he could just see shadows jumping around the fire. They looked like small demons then, fire breathing dragons.

"I've never heard of a fire-farting dragon, Captain." whispered one of the crew. The shadows were yelling at the pirates. They were yelling at the pirates to come back. All the pirates could see were the shadows next to the fire. As Jamie watched in fear, the shadows entered the sea. Hundreds of the Shee ran to the sea. Jamie could see only shadows. He thought that he was dealing with the devil himself.

Then here came the elephants and riders, Danny and Naughty in the lead. The turbulent water was splashing everywhere. They were going out to sea after the pirates.

Naughty caught up with the last boat. She kept screaming at the pirates who were in fear for their lives. Some were rowing and others were swinging their swords-all in vain; they could see nothing, too distracted to even notice the strange shadows. The captain was in the first boat. He was heading out to sea toward the ship when all the lanterns went out.

Naughty waited for more of the little people to get to the last boat. She quit screaming just as she and Danny were close enough to the two men in the back of the boat. Danny commanded, "Now!" Tinker and Doggy hit the two men with their trunks right across their faces. The two men flipped over the side. Danny and Naughty dropped back. This time some of the other little people started to rock the boat. The men stopped rowing to hold on, afraid of capsizing into the shark and shadow infested waters.

Then, without warning, two more men flew over the side. One of the men in the boat yelled, "The rest of you grab those oars and keep going!" This time Danny moved Tinker over to the stern of the boat. Tinker put her trunk up to the side of the last man's face. He could just see the long trunk as she stroked his face. He began to yell. No one had to knock him over, he just screamed and jumped over the side.

The rest of the men in the boat watched in horror. "We can't see the ship. How do we know where we are going?" No one knew what to do.

Then without warning, as many little people as the boat would hold were on the men.

The pirates had their long swords, but they could not see where to swing. All they could see were small, quick shadows running over the boat, like little demons, some screaming, stabbing, and taking on the pirates. Soon there were no pirates left on the boat. The boat drifted quietly in the night.

The second boat's crew were trying to hear what was going on with the last boat. But it was in vain. They could not see where they were going, and they could not hear the first boat with the captain over the screams of the Shee.

They sat still in the water trying to get a bearing. They could see the fire on the beach. And in the center of the island, they could see an orange glow. It looked like the island volcano, ready to go off at any time.

The middle boat was dead in the water, they were trying to look for the last boat. They yelled, but no answer.

One of the men was gone. He had disappeared over the side. After sudden silence boat was hit in every direction. There were shadows of little people all over the boat. They were too fast to fight. Some of the men jumped over the side, the ones that stayed wished they had jumped.

Just as quickly as the fight had started, it was over. The pirates in the boat looked surprised that they were still alive. They started to help some of the men back into the boat. Some of the men were wounded. As they helped each other into the boat, they wondered, "Why did the attack quit?" Then they could hear it. The sky was so dark that the weary pirates did not recognize that they had drifted south, almost into the fast water that ran between the two islands.

One of the pirates shakily ordered, "Grab the oars, row like you have never rowed before. Too late they realized they were caught in the stream; they were going out to sea, through the rocks and the coral. Rocks were now the problem and how to stay clear of them. They could not get out of the stream; they just had to ride the fast water as far as it took them. Captain LeDuval had no way of knowing that he was the only boat left. Somehow, he had made it to the ship in the darkness.

Ahoy there, Captain James. Can we come aboard?

CHAPTER 41

Jamie and the crew watched in horror as the shadows danced in the light of the fire. They swarmed the beach. They came out of nowhere. The biggest shadow could not be more than three feet tall. "What kind of place is this?" Jamie wondered.

The first mate shook his head in disbelief. "I have never seen anything like this before in my life. And I have seen many things. But this is something that I will never forget," he said as he was awe struck.

Then, Jamie watched as the shadows entered the sea, chasing the last boat. "Put out all the lamps. We don't want them to come out here," ordered Jamie.

"But what about Johnathan?" asked the first mate.

"I do not know if Johnathan is still alive. Let's wait and see. Put lookouts on all sides of the ship. All we can do is hope that Johnathan is safe." Jamie could hear the screams, hundreds of them coming from every direction at the same time. They were ear splitting, something unnatural. They were just high enough over the sea where they could see the Shee attack the last boat.

Even though they could not see very clearly, they knew no one was left. Jamie tried to see where the middle boat was, but it was too dark. They just waited and watched.

Then to the south of the ship they could hear more screaming. At first it was the Shee. Then it was the pirates' turn. Screaming and fighting, then quiet. By this time the clouds were starting to pass, and the moonlight finally was coming through the clouds. Jamie pointed over to the south. There was a boat being swept away in the fast water. "It looks like the ocean will take care of that one. Now where is Johnathan?" Jamie asked out loud to no one.

CHAPTER 42

Johnathan could hear Hairy whimpering. He ran over close to the jungle and dragged him back to where he had been sitting. He sat on the edge of the jungle holding Hairy. He'd had the wind knocked out of him. Hairy put his head on Johnathan's lap, watching intently. Wave after wave of Shee attacked the pirates. Just as Cahir had said, they drove them into the sea. Naughty and Danny were riding Doggy and Tinker. Right into the sea they went after the boats. It was too dark to see what was going on. By this time Johnathan could see the lights on the inside of the island. Even the sky glowed on the bottom of clouds from the light. Hairy and Johnathan sat and waited.

Then the screams stopped. They watched as the moonlight started to show through the no longer ominous clouds. Then Naughty and Doggy were the first to come up on the beach. Danny and Tinker were not far behind. Soon hundreds of Shee were back.

Unknown to Johnathan, Keavy had been by his side all the time. Until she tapped him on the shoulder, he did not know she had been there.

"Is Hairy alright?" asked Keavy. "I think so."

Let's go, Johnathan; we can't do anything else here tonight. "Do you think Hairy can walk?"

Johnathan stood, "Come on Hairy." The shaken dog carefully stood up, his tail started to move, and they slowly went back to the village.

They all walked back, not a word to be said. The silence as they returned to the village was deafening. Tonight, there was no party. All the Shee were quiet and tired. There was a fire in the center of the village. All the leaders were sitting around waiting.

Soon Cahir and Keavy came and sat. "Tonight, we did what we had to do. Tomorrow, we have to get Johnathan back to his uncle. We have a plan." Keavy kept talking. "Johnathan, first and foremost, you can never tell what you have seen here. Do you understand?"

"Yes," answered Johnathan.

"Even when your uncle asks, you never saw us. You might have heard us, but you never have seen us. This is the most awful place that you have ever seen. You tell him that you heard the screams of the Banshee."

"What is a Banshee?" asked Johnathan.

"A being from the old country, Juverna. they will know. The less you know the better. Can you give us your word, Johnathan?"

"Yes, no one will ever know."

"We will take you back to the beach in the morning. Your uncle will see you and send a boat. And if we never see the pirates again it will be too soon for me." Then Keavy instructed, "Now, it is time for rest as tomorrow will be a big day. Get something to eat and sleep. For in the morning, we will be on the beach."

CHAPTER 43

"Ahoy, there." Jamie looked over the side. It was Captain LeDuval.

"Can we come aboard?" The pirate asked.

"Where is my nephew?" Jamie yelled.

Right here, said the pirate. He pointed at the bundle in the boat.

Jamie looked at his men. "Aim right at the captain, but wait till I tell you to fire. You show me my nephew, or my crew will cut you down. And by the way, your other two boats are gone. Show me my nephew, now!" Jamie ordered one of the men to shoot a hole in the bottom of the boat. A shot rang out, right at the feet of the pirate captain. The wood parted and water was coming in the boat. "You don't have much time; where is my nephew?" Jamie yelled impatiently.

"Now, Captain Jamie, little Squid is all right. I just was not sure we could trust you. You know what I mean. All the pirate things and such. Sometimes people get the wrong impression of us." The pirate captain was getting antsier by the moment.

"Where is Johnathan!" Jamie yelled.

"Is he in your boat? Open the bundle now or we open fire." Jamie was furious.

"Don't fire man, let me explain. We are unarmed," he said with a softer voice and a smile. Every time Captain LeDuval lied, he closed his good eye as he smiled. And he gave Jamie his cold but friendly smile. "Jamie, we have Johnathan, but not right here. We left him on the beach. He is alright. He seems to have made friends with the Shee. I can take you there as soon as the sun comes up. Can we come aboard? It starting to get just a little wet in the boat." This time the pirate was begging. Jamie looked at the first mate. "Send down the irons."

The pirate boat was sinking. "Put the irons on and my crew will lift you from your boat. The choice is yours." Jamie yelled down at the pirates. "Or drown." Then he turned and walked away. The pirates could not have been faster. As fast as they got the irons on, they were lifted onto the ship. Jamie looked at his first mate, "Keep your guard on them every second. One by one the pirates were lifted onto the deck. Jamie walked over as the last man came up; it was the captain. Then he turned and started to walk away.

LeDuval was on deck just a few feet from Jamie. He looked at Jamie and smiled. "I would like to thank you for giving your fellow sailors a lift," as he watched his boat sink. Jamie was walking away from the pirate when he spoke. Jamie stopped and turned.

"String them up on the mast with their feet just touching the deck. Then check them for weapons.

The crew lifted each man up by their irons. Then began looking for weapons.

Knives, pistols, daggers, hidden swords fell to the deck making loud clatter. Jamie looked at the first mate. "Unarmed, like hell." And walked to his cabin.

CHAPTER 44

This would be the last night Johnathan would spend with the Shee. He didn't remember if he went to sleep or not. As soon as he could see first light, they ate and left.

Keavy looked at Johnathan "You will be missed." She put her arms around him. As he looked into her eyes full of tears, he knew she was ready to cry. Then her eyes turned cold. "We will make sure that you make it safely back to your uncle. And, Johnathan, you might be leaving, but we will always be with you."

Cahir came up. "It is time for you to go."

Hairy and Johnathan went up the mountainside. Danny and Naughty were right with them. He could not see anyone else, but he felt that they were there. When they got to the top of the mountainside, they could see the ocean. The sky was deep cobalt blue. The sand glowed with a pink, almost red shine. This was truly the happiest island he had seen. And how beautiful it is when thinking about the little people who live here. Naughty handed Johnathan his last broad leaf. Hairy was ready to jump in.

"Where are Tinker and Doggy?"

"They could not come this time," said Naughty. "Are you ready to go?" Into the water they went. Wanting the ride never to end, it was the quickest that Johnathan had gone around the mountain waterslide. When they reached the west side of the slide, they got off. He could see out to the ocean. There was Uncle Jamie coming to the shore. He was in the first boat.

"Johnathan!" Danny yelled. "Look in the second boat, pirates!"

Hairy started to growl. Johnathan put his hand on Hairy, "It is all right," he soothed him.

Naughty looked at the boy. "Let's go down and meet them." They cautiously went down the path to the beach and waited for the boats.

CHAPTER 45

At first light, Jamie was on the deck. “Have you seen anything of the boy?” He asked the men.

“No, sir,” came the reply.

“Lower the boats. It is time we went to shore.” Jamie watched the pirates as he talked. There were only about ten left, plus the captain. “Put them in a boat,” Jamie said.

Captain LeDuval smiled and nodded his head. “We will help you find Squid; we are somewhat attached to him. It will be nice to see him again.” Jamie took the boats right where there had been a fire on the beach last night. Jamie could hear a dog barking. One of Jamie’s men said, “Captain, look over there, it is a dog running on the beach!

Then right behind the dog was Johnathan.

“Uncle Jamie, Uncle Jamie!”

Jamie stood up in the boat. “Johnathan,” he called back, so relieved to see his nephew that his voice nearly trembled. The boats could not go fast enough, it seemed like it took years before they were going to get there. But they finally did. Jamie jumped into the water. He could not wait any longer. He swam to the shore. He grabbed the barefoot boy before the boats made it to the shore. Behind Jamie, he heard a growl. Hairy did not like anyone picking up the boy.

“Now who is this,” laughed Jamie, not giving the dog a second glance.

“Uncle Jamie, meet Hairy, he is my dog.” The second boat came on the shore. Hairy was ready to attack when he saw the pirates. His hair stood up and his teeth were showing. Hairy was growling, not in a friendly way.

“Uncle Jamie, Hairy does not like the pirates.” Jamie was laughing as he held Johnathan, “Well, I like this dog already. Johnathan, how?

How did you do it?" Jamie was not going to put his nephew down for anything. By now, the crew was on the beach. Jamie told the first mate to send some of the men back to the ship, keep a few men, and get fresh water and fruit for the ship.

"Over here Johnathan," It was Naughty calling. Johnathan walked over to the edge of the jungle to see what she wanted. "We have all the fruit that you will need. It is all here. Cahir put it here this morning, and right behind this row of trees is fresh water. We don't want Uncle Jamie wandering all over the island," said Naughty.

"I will miss you," Johnathan said.

"Just call your uncle over here before his men go into the jungle." Naughty smiled. Then disappeared.

"Uncle Jamie, come over here, please," yelled Johnathan. Jamie walked over; when he saw the fruit, he looked at the boy but did not say a word.

"Uncle, over here, look." Jamie pushed his way past the trees to see the freshwater pond and waterfall.

Jamie yelled back at the men. "Over here, come and see what Johnathan has for us." Jamie laughed and put his hands on his hips. "And to think that I was worried about you."

Just then the sound of a canon came from the ship.

Right behind the men were the screams of the Shee.

Johnathan yelled, "Naughty!" and ran for the jungle, Jamie right behind. But no one was there.

Jamie looked back at the ship as the skull and crossbones flag went up the mast.

CHAPTER 46

The second boat was caught in the fast water. Out to sea they sped. Some of the men were wounded, blood pooled everywhere. All they could do was hang on. The rest of the men tried to push off the rocks as best as they could. One of the pirates took charge and kept shouting orders. They hit one rock after the other. The boat sounded like it was going to break up at any time. Many of the pirates could not swim and were afraid of capsizing or being killed by the rocks. They sailed on in the darkness. When they finally reached the end of the fast water, they just collapsed. Too tired to go any farther and it was too dark to see anyway. The clouds passed and they could see by the moonlight. They drifted until daylight.

"Let's go," shouted the new pirate leader. And he pointed toward the direction of the island. The boat was taking on a little sea water, not a happy thought. Considering what they had just gone through, that was not too bad. "Keep rowing and the rest of you start bailing out the boat before we sink," said the man in charge. Some of the men grumbled, "Who made him the captain?"

Then all around the boat were sharks. More than a person could count. Everyone was bailing about this time. The sharks could smell the blood from the wounded and more were congregating for the pirate buffet. The new captain said, "If there is anyone who is not able to do his share and bail, Throw him over the side."

Now the men were bailing harder than ever, actually bailing as though their lives depended on their success.

They could see Jamie's ship. It looked like no one was on it. Then they could see three boats headed for the shore. Stay on this side of the ship. That way the others will not see us. As the boat came closer to the ship, they could hear men talking. "Quiet now," one of the pirates said as they came along the side of the ship. Ever so quiet they scaled the side of the ship. They could only see about five of the crew. But the rest of the pirates were shackled on the main deck. One of the pirates on the deck saw his fellow pirates coming over the rail. The new leader put his finger over his mouth as if to say be quiet. Jamie's crew were watching the shore. Johnathan had just run over to Jamie. This was the high point of the day, but that was about to end.

The pirates swarmed the deck. There was no chance for the crew. Not a shot was fired. As soon as it started, it was over. One of the crew was stabbed and fell over the side. The sharks that had followed the boat to the ship made quick work of the man. Now the tables had turned; Jamie's crew were in irons and the pirates were in control of the ship. There were more crew below deck who were swiftly put in irons with the others.

"Give me the glass," ordered the new leader. He raised the glass to the shoreline. "Well, we still have a captain. Ready one gun and fire a round next to the jungle. That will let them know we are in control of the ship." The cannon fired. The shot went over the heads of the men and to the left, on the edge of the jungle.

The next event was a Jolly Rodger hoisted up the mast of *The Fighting Dove.*

CHAPTER 47

Cahir was watching Johnathan and Jamie. He turned and said to Keavy, "We have done a very good thing today.

"Why, Cahir, are you going soft on me?" Keavy smiled. Just then a cannonball whistled toward them. It exploded right behind Keavy. She was thrown right into Cahir's arms. She was visible and bleeding. Cahir ran for the jungle, carrying his mate. All the Shee followed. Johnathan was running toward them but stopped as his uncle caught him. Johnathan was crying.

Cahir laid Keavy down next to the stream at the top of the mountain. Some of the other women were taking over for him.

"Cahir, we will take care of Keavy. She will be fine, now go and do what you must."

Cahir bent down and gave Keavy a kiss on the head, "I must go."

Keavy smiled, "You take care of Johnathan. Make sure that he leaves with his uncle. I will be right here when you get back. Be careful, my love. But I think it is time that the pirates do not cause harm to anyone again."

Cahir nodded, "Now we are at war!" And away he ran down the jungle, followed by hundreds of the Shee. This time the jungle swayed as the invisible stampede moved to the shore. Cahir was down the mountain in the blink of an eye. All the Shee were at the edge of the jungle. "Naughtia, (a name her father only used to tell her something important) go tell Johnathan to come here and bring his uncle."

"But, father," she interrupted.

"Just do as I told you. I have a plan."

Naughty went up to Johnathan. She was right behind him. Naughty reached out and touched Johnathan on the shoulder. "Johnathan, come over to the edge of the jungle and bring your uncle. We will be waiting."

Captain LeDuval smiled as he looked back at Jamie. Jamie ordered, "Keep him on the ground; if the pirate moves kill him."

Johnathan knew that Naughty was up to something, "Uncle Jamie, come with me, I must show you something."

"Not now, "Johnathan," he said.

"Uncle Jamie, look at me."

Jamie turned, with a surprised look. "I must show you something; follow me to the jungle."

Jamie told his men, "Stand fast. I will be right back." And he followed Johnathan to the jungle's edge. "Johnathan, I don't see how this is a good time for a walk, we have a ship to get back."

"Uncle Jamie, I would like you to meet Naughty; she is a friend of mine.

Jamie watched as a greenish three-foot girl was suddenly in front of him.

"Captain, you have a very brave nephew; you should be very proud. I would like for you to talk to my father Cahir. He is our leader." Jamie looked, but no one was visible. Naughty said, "Look again."

This time Jamie could not say a thing. "My name is Cahir, and I will take your ship back with your help. But you have to give me your word that you will never speak of this place and of the Shee. Do I have your word?" Jamie nodded his head. He still did not believe what he was seeing.

Johnathan took his uncle's arm. "Uncle, they saved me many times. They are my friends. If not for them, I would not be here.

Jamie looked at Cahir, "What could you do that I cannot? You are so small. Cahir gave Jamie a disappointed look. He turned and waved his hand. The entire jungle was filled with Shee. Then they were gone. "Johnathan will explain later. But for now, we have a ship to take. Do I have your word?"

Jamie said, "You have my word, and many thanks for saving and caring for my nephew." The two shook hands, one large hand and one small hand, but both were strong.

"Let the pirate captain go. Have all of your men sit on the beach. Whatever you do, don't get up. Do you understand?"

Jamie said, "Yes, but why?"

"Just sit and watch. We are counting on the pirate to take all the boats. Let him tie them together and go back to the ship. We will do the rest.

"Ahoy, there! called a man from the ship. We will let your crew members go if you let our captain come back to the ship."

Captain LeDuval turned and looked at Jamie. With his smile he said, "Captain, I will guarantee your men's safety to the shore. Now I will have to take all the boats so your crew can return."

Jamie told the men, "Untie the pirate." The men protested, but Jamie again said, "Untie the captain. Let him leave with the boats. Now move!"

Jamie's men did so, but they resented what they were doing by letting Captain LeDuval go free. "Everyone, come here now," ordered Jamie. "Everyone, sit on the sand now! Whatever happens, do not get up, understand?" The men sat. They looked a little frightened. "Don't get up!" instructed Jamie.

"Thank you, kind sir," said Captain LeDuval as he started to tie the boats together.

Jamie and his men watched as the pirate was preparing to go back to the ship. Then all around the crew from of The Fighting Dove were footprints. They just kept coming from the jungle. They went right to the boats. Jamie could see the boats going lower and lower in the water. There must have been hundreds of the Shee in them. And the pirate captain did not even know they were in his boat.

Jamie said in a low voice, "Be steady, men, and watch. Whatever happens now is not up to us." Jamie reached over to Johnathan and put his arm around him. Hairy was wagging his tail. He was not worried. The crew sat there and watched.

Johnathan knew what was going to happen.

By the time the LeDuval reached the ship, he was exhausted. "How could three empty boats feel so heavy," he thought. The crew had let the nets down on the side of the ship. As soon as the boats touched the ship, the nets were moving. Hundreds of Shee were up to the deck before the captain had tied off. He watched the nets move. "What is this?" he thought out loud. He put his finger up to see if there was any wind. Then he smiled and went up the side to greet his crew.

"The warmest of welcomes to you, sir," said Captain Duval's first mate. Do you like your new ship?"

"You mates did well, I am right proud of you all." The captain smiled and looked at Jamie's crew on the deck.

"What should we do with them?" asked the first mate.

"Throw them over the side. But take the irons off them as we may need those restraints later. Those irons would kill a good shark if it swallowed them." He smiled and started to walk over to the chart room. The pirates started walking over toward Jamie's men.

"It is time for your swim," said one of the pirates to Jamie's crew. The pirate crew stopped in their tracks. The mast and rigging started to go dark with the shadows of the Shee moving up them.

"Did you hear that, it sounded like a scream?" As they looked around, a man at the top of the rigging screamed. It looked as if he was floating over to the side. Then he fell into the sea with his throat cut. Captain LeDuval was back on deck. To his amazement, his crew were being slaughtered right where they stood in front of him. He drew his sword, but all there were mere shadows in the light. Then he could see some of the eyes of the Shee reflected in the light. He was horrified. The ropes were swinging down with no one on them. But each time an empty rope would come down, a pirate fell. And the battle screams were somehow different than the screams on the beach. Before, they gave a warning. Now it was the cry of death. All of Jamie's crew would have jumped ship if they were not shackled to the deck. All they could do was hold their ears and pray.

Within minutes of the arrival of the Shee, all of the pirate crew were dead, by every means possible. The only one left was their captain, LeDuval.

The shadows picked up every pirate and took them to the side of the ship's rail. One after the other, whether they were dead or alive, the Shee tossed them into the ocean. It was a very good day indeed for the sharks on that side of the boat. The shadows, all of them, engulfed LeDuval. Jamie's crew could see only darkness. The Shee had removed all of his weapons. One Shee was on Captain LeDuval's back with a blade on to his neck, two others had tied his hands. They were hanging from each side of him. They made him kneel on the deck.

"Come out and show yourself," the captain ordered.

The shadows opened enough for a path as Cahir walked in front of the pirate, "As for your days destruction, they have come to an end. We are everywhere that the wind blows. People like you forced us from our home in Juverna. We have been pushed all over the world; it stops here and stops now. From this day forward, whenever we see the strong hurting the weak, we will be there."

Cahir was now visible. "Do you have any last words, LeDuval?"

"You, green little pile of poop, who are you?"

"WE ARE THE SHEE!" Cahir pointed to the boats. The only noise now was the crew of The Fighting Dove, wondering if they were next. The hundreds of shadows picked the pirate captain up, and carried him to the side of the ship, to the long boats. They covered him like bees in a hive, all the way down to the boats. LeDuval lay in the bottom of the boat as the oars rowed the boats back to the shore seeming like they were alive. LeDuval was soaked from the waist down, and it was not seawater.

Cahir walked up to Jamie's crew. "Don't ever tell anyone of what you have seen here;" then Naughty let out screams to end all screams. The last of the Shee took the chains off two of Jamie's crew before they left with the boats. And the crew freed the rest of the crew as the Shee left the ship. The boats quietly rowed toward the island. Most of the Dove's crew were free now and watched as the boats rowed themselves to the shore. There was a fire on the beach now. The crew watched as the crafts arrived at the shoreline. Then the shadows of the day carried LeDuval from the boats to the fire.

Jamie waited as the pirate was dropped at his feet. "Thank you, my friends," he said quietly.

Johnathan watched as the flag came down. Everyone was cheering as The Fighting Dove's colors were restored.

"Johnathan, I think that you might have a few stories to tell."

"Yes, Uncle Jamie, but I told Cahir and Keavy that I would not."

This day was almost done. The boats were almost here. Jamie looked at Hairy, "What are we going to tell your father and mother about Hairy?"

"Tell them that he is my friend, Uncle." Then Johnathan put his arms around Uncle Jamie, "I think Hairy is smiling. Would you like to go home, Hairy?" asked Johnathan.

Hairy tried to talk as best as he could while his tail wagged happily. I think that was a yes," smiled Jamie.

The boats were at the beach. One of the sailors came up to Jamie. "Captain, I can't tell you what happened. But the pirates are gone for good."

Jamie smiled, "Don't worry, it will be all right. Besides no one would believe you anyway."

Jamie instructed the men, "Load the fruit and water into the boats. We have to get Johnathan home to his father and mother."

"Aye, aye, sir," came a cheerful reply.

"Cahir was now next to Jamie and Johnathan. "You must go now. Johnathan, we will miss you. And you, Captain, thank you. I know that you will keep your word. Maybe we will meet again."

Uncle Jamie smiled at Cahir. "I owe you much. Thank you."

"You must go now," then Cahir was gone.

As Johnathan walked to the boats, his uncle reached down and picked him up. "Johnathan, you have grown. You are almost too big to carry." They were both laughing, as they headed back to the ship.

CHAPTER 48

Before nightfall, they were on their way. Sadly, Uncle Jamie had lost some good men. When they got back, he and his brother would have to see their families and tell them what good men they were and compensate the families for their loved one's loss and services.

For the first time in weeks, Johnathan realized that all he had on was a torn pair of shorts and what was left of a shirt. Hairy and Johnathan stood with Uncle Jamie watching the Caribbean sunset. The sun had rays coming from all around it as it set close to the horizon. There were just enough clouds to light up the lower sky with red and gold fireworks.

"We will make good time Johnathan; we have the wind and the weather."

Johnathan didn't know how many days it took to get back, but this was the greatest adventure he had ever had. He already missed his new friends and at the same time, he was eager to see his home and family. "Johnathan, sorry I missed your birthday." Jamie put his arm around the not as little boy.

"Uncle Jamie, I didn't know I had one," The two of them, all the way home, spent each night watching the sunsets.

Then early one morning Johnathan was on deck when the lookout shouted, "Land Ho."

Uncle Jamie came over to the rail, looking to the top of the mountain, pointing. Johnathan looked but could not see anything.

Jamie walked over to where Johnathan was standing and said, "Here, look through this glass." He took the glass; right on top of the mountain was his mother waving and jumping right next to his father. "Uncle Jamie! How did they know I was safe?"

"Johnathan," Jamie laughed. "Look what the crew made for you." He pointed up. On the highest mast was a white flag. Made from Johnathan's shirt, with a big J on it for Johnathan, flying in the wind. Johnathan waved as hard as he could and Hairy was barking as loud as he could.

"Uncle Jamie," said Johnathan. "I miss my friends. Do you ever think we will ever see them again?"

"I don't know son," Jamie replied quietly. "I just don't know."

Then Johnathan's hand felt cold. He looked down at his hand. But could not see it. "You never know Johnathan, anything can happen." Naughty was right next to him. Then she was gone.

The guns at the fort let off a full barrage in honor of the return of The Fighting Dove.

Johnathan grinned as they sailed around the south side of the island to the harbor town. The entire town was there cheering. Welcome back.

CHAPTER 49

Cahir ran as fast as he could back to the home of the Shee. Keavy was resting on her bed, waiting for his return. Cahir slowly put his hand on her.

"Is Johnathan all right?"

"Yes, he is with his uncle."

"Did we lose anyone, Cahir?"

"No, we know where they are."

"Danny and Naughtia?" Keavy asked, with a smile.

"Yes, and a few others. They went with Johnathan, for another adventure."

"I thought that might happen. How about Captain LeDuval?"

"He will never be the same."

"Johnathan's uncle took him back to pay for his crimes. Some of the Shee are with him, as we speak."

Captain LeDuval was in the brig of The Fighting Dove. "Who is there, show yourself." He kept asking, over and over. His pants continued to stay wet. As he twitched and shook.

The End

Captain Jamie James	Captain of The Fighting Dove
Johnathan James	Jamie's nephew
John James	Johnathan's father
Maria James	Johnathan's mother
The Fighting Dove's flag	Blue with a dove holding a canon
First mate on the Dove	Christian
Naughtia or Naughty	Daughter of Keavy & Cahir
Danny	Son of Keavy & Cahir
Danny's pet	Tinker
Naughty's pet	Doggy
Keavy	Danny & Naughty's mother
Cahir	Danny & Naughty's Father
Feme	Young woman
Oillin	Elf
Conan	Hound or wolf
Juverna	Ireland
Aed	Dragon (fire)
Aga	Dragon (contentious, warlike)

Pirate Captain	LeDuval (the Devil)
Mr. Jon	Pirate navigator
Wink	Pirate
Dirty	Pirate
Smoll	Pirate that hit Johnathan

Printed in the USA
CPSIA information can be obtained
at www.ICGtesting.com
JSHW021142190224
57603JS00001B/1

9 798893 303186